Sounds of Murder

A Pamela Barnes Acoustic Mystery

by

Patricia Rockwell

For information, email **Cozy Cat Press**, cozycatpress@aol.com or visit our website at: www.cozycatpress.com

COZY CAT
P R E S S

LCCN: 2010922640
ISBN: 978-0-9844795-0-4
Printed in the United States of America

Cover design by Scott Saunders of *Design 7 Studio*, www.design7studio.com

PUBLISHER'S NOTE: The publisher is not responsible for any adverse reactions to eating any of the dishes created from the recipes contained in this book.

10 9 8 7 6 5 4 3 2 1

Dedicated to Milt, my own personal "Rocky."

Chapter 1

It was getting dark and the wind was picking up when Pamela Barnes roared into the small parking lot on the side of Blake Hall on the campus at Grace University. Barely missing nicking the tail light on Dr. Swinton's old Buick, she found one remaining spot at the far end just minutes before her graduate seminar was scheduled to start at 6 p.m. She was just locking her Civic, when her graduate assistant, Kent Drummond, appeared.

"Hi, Dr. B," he greeted her, his ear stud gleaming in the last rays of sunlight. "Got the last space, I see."

"Yes," she smiled. "Lucky me." She tightened her jacket around her body. The wind snapped her fine blonde hair briskly in front of her face. Kent stepped beside her and the two of them strode purposefully towards the side entrance of the building.

"Those were some hard articles you assigned for tonight, Dr. B," he noted, holding the door open for her as Pamela zipped inside before another gust of wind whipped up her skirt.

"It's graduate school," explained Pamela, laughing. "You don't expect it to be easy, do you?" Kent chuckled weakly in response.

"Come on, Dr. B," he moaned, "Those articles were overkill." Pamela registered his word choice with amusement. Kent's all black outfit with a blood-spattered machete design on the front of his t-shirt would never scream "conscientious graduate student" to the rest of the world, but she knew his "look" was all bravado. He was one of her best students.

"That's material you're going to have to know," responded Pamela.

"If you say so. Oh, Dr. B, I ran that second group of subjects through the protocol. You want me to enter the data tonight?" he asked, his sneakers squishing as he walked.

"You mean they all showed?"

Their footsteps echoed in the high-ceilinged main hallway of the ancient old building.

"Sure thing, Dr. B. That's what extra credit in a hard course like Dr. Clark's will do for your turn-out," he chirped. How true, she thought. Charlotte Clark was famous and with fame came popularity. Students across campus wanted to take her courses on addiction, whether they were Psych majors or not. And Charlotte always made her students participate in research. Too bad she didn't allow them to participate in animal psych research too. Then her friend Arliss, who taught animal psychology, could benefit from Charlotte's largess. However, Pamela was not going to look a gift horse in the mouth. She would use her participants however she got them.

She turned to the young man beside her, saying, "You can hold off on data entry until tomorrow. Then, changing the subject, she added, "Kent, are you sure you locked the lab up properly when you left this afternoon?"

"Sure, Dr. B," he answered, "I'm always very careful with the lab."

"That's good," she replied, sounding a note of caution. "We can't be too careful, really. That lab has some of the most expensive equipment on campus or even in the state. I'm sure there are plenty of people who'd like to get their hands on it." She hated playing campus cop like this, but her Chair had been pounding the faculty lately about lab security.

"Like I said, Dr. B," he repeated, "You can count on me. I always lock it when I leave and I double check to make sure all the equipment is put away and safe too. Don't worry." Kent waved good-bye and trekked across the hall towards the seminar room on the right.

Pamela noticed her colleague Phineas Ottenback coming out of the departmental office across the hallway on the left. He locked the door behind himself.

"Oh, Dr. Barnes," he said turning, eyes popping open as he saw Pamela, "Did you need to get into the office? I'm sorry I just locked it." A shock of wispy, red hair flopped down over his forehead.

"That's all right, Phineas," she responded. She thought it amusing that Phineas was always so formal, even when there were no students around. "I'm on my way to my seminar. I assume you're on your way to class too."

"Oh, yes, upstairs." he said, in that quaint, nasal voice that Pamela found just slightly irritating. As he started towards the large central staircase further down the hallway, he suddenly turned back to her.

"Oh, Dr. Barnes, " he confided, "You're on the Tenure Committee, aren't you?"

"Yes, Phineas," she sputtered, "but...but I can't, in good conscience, discuss anything about the committee or its procedures with you, seeing as how you're a candidate."

"Yes, Dr. Barnes," he said, hesitating, "but, I was just wondering if I...about the possibility of ...what you would think if someone removed their name from consideration for tenure?"

"Phineas," she responded, "You surely wouldn't want to do that. I mean, I can't say anything officially, but I believe your chances of getting tenure are as good as the other two candidates. I really can't and shouldn't even say that." She now felt horrible for even having this conversation with the man. Tenure was a serious and private matter. It was a make or break moment for young faculty members such as Phineas. Get tenure and you had a job for life. Be denied tenure and you were essentially fired.

"It's just a thought, you know," Phineas said, "I was only wondering what would happen—hypothetically--if someone were to drop out of the running, so to speak..." He pulled himself from deep thought with a strange jerky motion and suddenly changed the topic. "Anyway, thank you very much, Dr. Barnes, for your honesty. I would appreciate it if you wouldn't mention this conversation to anyone."

"Of course not, Phineas," she answered, befuddled. He took her hand gingerly and shook it very formally, then quickly headed up the central staircase without another word.

How strange. She hadn't studied the tenure portfolios for the Psychology Department's three candidates yet. She needed to get down to Charlotte's office—Charlotte was Chair of the Tenure Committee—and study the files. But from what she knew of Phineas' work, he would likely be granted tenure. He and his research partner, Rex Tyson, churned out several solid articles each year in top-notch journals, and tenure decisions were typically based on research productivity. It didn't make sense for Phin to even contemplate removing his name from consideration for tenure.

She stood there, staring after him for a moment. Then, selecting her key to the department's main office from her key ring, she quickly opened the glass-windowed door and entered the darkened insides. Just a narrow beam of light from the hallway illuminated the faculty mailboxes on the wall. As she reached into her cubby hole for her mail, she heard voices coming from the office of the Department Head, Mitchell Marks, which was located through a second small office where the departmental secretary worked.

Pamela stood frozen as the two voices rang out behind Mitchell's closed door. It was unusual for Mitchell to be in his office this late in the day. Pamela couldn't make out the gist of what was apparently an argument, but it soon became clear to her who the combatants were—obviously Mitchell, the Head of Grace University's Psychology Department, and, no surprise to Pamela, Charlotte Clark, the department's prima donna, star grant-getter, and world-renown expert on addiction. Pamela cocked her ear closer to the intervening office door, trying to decipher the cause of the fight.

"For God's sake, Mitchell," she heard Charlotte Clark bellow. "I've brought this department millions of dollars in research funding, a beautiful state-of-the-art experimental computer lab, and hoards of fame. The Dean had damn well better consider that, and the multi-million dollar grants I've brought and will bring to Grace University."

"Now, Charlotte, calm down," said Marks. It was a request, not an order.

"Don't try to calm me down, Mitchell!" Charlotte yelled. "Remember, I have tenure so I don't have to do his bidding. And I'm not some boot licker like the rest of this gutless faculty," she said, "not wanting to jeopardize an upcoming promotion or book deal. I can say what I think. And what I think is that this entire department is full of cowards. And Mitchell—you're the worst of the lot, the biggest coward of them all. You let the Dean walk all over you. It's time somebody stood up to him. All you care about is avoiding conflict. But I don't care about avoiding anything and I'm going to give him a piece of my mind."

Pamela could hear Charlotte's voice getting louder as she came closer to the door, then, evidently, turning back to Mitchell as he called out to her.

"Charlotte, for heaven's sake, don't do that!"

"Just try and stop me!" Charlotte screamed back at him, and her voice suddenly became even louder as she opened the door between Mitchell's office and the secretary's office. Pamela could see the outline of her body highlighted in the door frame. Charlotte was a striking, middle-aged woman, with a beautifully styled head of blonde curls. Her designer suit and Monolo Blahnik heels looked elegant enough to be featured on the cover of Vogue. As she turned to leave, she tossed a final comment over her shoulder:

"And, Mitchell, you can forget that stupid Chili Cook-Off of yours that you so foolishly think of as a departmental fundraiser. I won't be participating this year!"

As Charlotte's footsteps stormed toward her, Pamela quickly grabbed her mail and headed out the main office door and across the hall toward the seminar room. She slipped into the room just as she heard Charlotte slam the main office door shut and storm down the hallway. The last thing she wanted was to get in the way of an angry Charlotte Clark steam-rolling in her direction.

What in the world had caused such a fight between Charlotte and their Chair? And where was Charlotte going now in such a huff? To the Dean as she'd threatened? And if so, what for? She'd love to be able to find out, but Pamela was sure the gossip mill would supply the answer tomorrow.

Right now, she had to concentrate on conducting her Tuesday night graduate seminar in acoustics. She looked around the room. She could smell the old wood paneling and the faint scent of leather in the worn, but comfortable arm chairs situated around the long conference table.

Kent had positioned himself in his favorite location on the side of the table near the windows. Two girls were already in the room and were talking to Kent. He was cheerfully responding to their eager questions. Luckily, it appeared the students had not heard the horrific argument between Mitchell and Charlotte that had just occurred across the hall.

Pamela went quickly and quietly to the end of the long table at the front of the room and sat down. Then she began to review the articles she'd assigned her class—the impossibly hard ones according to Kent--while she waited for her class to arrive.

Soon, three more female students and three male students arrived and Pamela began the class. In no time at all she had forgotten—well, almost forgotten—Charlotte Clark and her tirade in Mitchell's office.

"Okay, class," she announced, rising and getting their attention, "you read three articles about acoustics for tonight's class. Who can tell me, in a nutshell, what these articles had in common, and how they were different from each other?"

One girl quickly raised her hand.

"Dr. Barnes," she declared, "Those articles were very technical, more than any other articles you've assigned. Truthfully, I was lost." She looked a bit sheepish, until several other students chimed in, in agreement.

"Let's look at it this way," responded Pamela. "Eventually you'll need to understand how to use the acoustic technology described in these articles if you intend to find careers using sound analysis. You won't necessarily need to understand how the technology works. Even so, it's a good idea to start with a discussion of the workings of a piece of equipment with which you'll all need to become very familiar—the spectrograph." She stopped and looked around the room. Everyone looked a bit terrified.

"Consider this," she said, turning to the chalkboard and taking a piece of chalk and dragging it firmly down the board, making that unmistakable sound that makes a person's teeth clench. The class cringed noticeably.

"Now," she asked, turning back to them. "What was that?"

"Torture!" yelled one blond man near the door. The class laughed in relief.

"In addition to torture?" asked Pamela.

"I'd call it—just noise," ventured one young woman sitting close to Pamela's end of the table.

"Just noise?" Pamela prompted.

"Yeah," added another male near the far end of the table, close to the door.

"So, what is noise?" she asked. In her mind, she couldn't help but recall the noisy shouting match she had witnessed just moments ago in the main office. She was still mystified by its severity and its reason. Charlotte was notoriously hot tempered, but this was the angriest she had ever heard her--so angry, in fact, that Mitchell had seemed almost overwhelmed by her fury.

Another young woman raised her hand. Pamela nodded towards her.

"I'd say that noise is a sound that isn't attractive."

"And," continued Pamela, "what constitutes 'attractive'?"

The class was seemingly stumped. Pamela waited. Then, she picked up one of the assigned articles.

"If you remember in this article, the author presents a rather detailed discussion of the difference between 'sound' and 'noise.' Would anyone like to describe that difference?" No one raised their hand.

"All right. Here's where all that technology comes in." She turned to the chalkboard and drew a wavy, measured line, and next to it, a very choppy, disjointed line of the same length. "What did I draw?" she asked.

A tentative hand peeked up over an open textbook.

"Helen?"

"I believe those are drawings of a vowel and chalk being scraped over a chalkboard." She smiled sweetly at Pamela.

"That's actually more detailed than even I was hoping for, Helen. Bravo! I'm just guessing at the vowel or screeching chalk characteristics of these two masterful paintings I've just created for you."

The class giggled. She liked to make them laugh. All teachers, she realized had a bit of stand-up comic in them. Even so, she was quite good at covering her true feelings when she lectured—and right now her true feelings were centered on the battle she had overheard earlier in the main office.

"What makes the first drawing different from the second?" she asked.

"The first one is smooth and regular and the second one is all over the place," said one young man.

"Right," answered Pamela. "The first one is regular; it forms a pattern, just as does any ..."   She looked directly at the girl who'd brought up the "attractive" argument. "Just as does any attractive sound, such as speech. The second drawing is erratic; it has no regular pattern—it's the pattern of noise."

The class contemplated this distinction for a while. The old analog clock on the wall audibly ticked off the seconds.

"Now," said Pamela, "let's take a look at some other characteristics of speech--our patterned sound."

She drew another wavy line on the board.

"Let's assume," she said, "that this is the acoustic output for a portion of speech. We have sophisticated software that can analyze many acoustic features of speech and other sounds--even of noise." She smiled and they all laughed.

"Let's say that this wavy line represents the word 'cat.'" She pointed to the line and she then added a horizontal and a vertical axis. "Now, what types of features of a speaker's voice can we possibly determine by looking at this acoustic output?"

A hand rose. "I believe if the word begins on the left and ends on the right of the line, that you could measure how long it took the speaker to say the word."

"Absolutely right," announced Pamela. "That is, this acoustic wave provides us a measure of time--how long it takes to produce a sound or sounds. What else?" She looked around the room, hoping for someone else to volunteer.

Kent raised his hand.

"Mr. Drummond?" she asked.

"Not sure here, Dr. B., but I think the height of the wave is a measure of how loud the sound is."

"Right again!" she claimed. "Excellent, class! It appears you did read those impossible to understand articles after all. The height of the wave is a measure of the sound's amplitude or intensity--or in layman's terms--loudness." She drew some dramatically larger wave forms and some dramatically smaller forms and demonstrated the difference in their loudness.

"There's one more feature you can extract from looking at this form. Anyone know what it is?" she coaxed.

"Dr. Barnes, please don't jump on me if this is wrong," offered the shy girl who had hidden behind her book, "but I think the third feature you're looking for is the number of waves within a certain space."

"Yes, Peggy," said Pamela, "and what do we call that?"

"I think it's pitch--or rather—frequency," responded the girl.

"A perfect score for my brilliant class," announced Pamela. The students were all looking around the room, smiling and proud. Maybe, some were hoping, the "brilliant" label would continue through until final grades. That's what she loved about graduate students; they often didn't trust their own instincts and they needed good instincts to be linguists or have careers in acoustic technology—as many of them wanted. She knew that. You had to be able to listen to sound and extract meaning from it other than just the words--like the words she'd heard shot back and forth between Charlotte and Mitchell earlier. Now what meaning could she derive from that interchange? From the volume? The tempo? The pitch?

"Yes," continued Pamela, "what we perceive as pitch is really the number of waves or frequency of waves within a certain space. That is, a high pitched sound," and Pamela sang a very high note, "would have far more waves within a certain space," and she drew many evenly spaced waves together, "than a low pitched sound," and she sang a low note, "which would have the waves longer and spread out more like this" and she drew in the same space, fewer evenly spaced waves together.

Pamela continued to explain acoustic technology and soon, before she realized it, several hours had whizzed by. With some final words and an explanation of next week's reading assignment, she dismissed the class for the evening. As she was gathering her belongings, she called to Kent to come over.

"Kent," she said, "please, don't consider me an old fogy, but would you be so kind as to go down and check on the lab one more time? Just be sure it's locked."

"Sure, Dr. B.," he answered, "I'm on my way." He headed out the door, taking his book sack with him. Pamela followed the last few students out the door, and then turned and closed the seminar door. This door, she mused, didn't need to be locked because there wasn't anything in this room of value--at least not of value to most thieves who were looking for equipment and devices that they could sell readily on the black market. The department was more than worried about possible theft in their multi-million dollar computer lab, but the rest of the old dilapidated building contained little worth stealing. She headed down the hallway towards the lab and the parking lot entrance. Just then, Kent came running back towards her from the lab, yelling.

"Dr. Barnes! Dr. Barnes!" he screamed, "Come quick! Come to the lab! It's horrible! Hurry!"

Chapter 2

Pamela followed Kent, running behind him around the corner of the main hallway towards the experimental computer laboratory at the far end of the side hallway. She could see in the distance that the door to the lab was wide open and the lights were on. Kent ran through the doorway and Pamela followed on his heels. He went immediately to the first row of computer carrels, to Carrel #4, one of the department's special "souped up" computers. Pamela could see a woman in the carrel bent over the computer desk, a tousled head of blonde curls. As she drew closer, she realized that the woman was Charlotte Clark.

"It's Dr. Clark," said Kent, "Dr. Barnes! I think she's dead!"

Pamela's heart seemed to stop beating as she froze in place, staring at Charlotte, who was seated, bent over the desk. She saw immediately that the power cord from a set of headphones was wrapped tightly around her neck, the headphones themselves hanging uselessly down the side of Charlotte's neck. The side of Charlotte's face was tinged grayish-blue.

"Oh, my God!" Pamela whispered, suddenly digging in her purse on her shoulder. After a few seconds of scrounging, she located her cell phone and tapped in the number for the campus police. The call was answered immediately.

"Please," she spoke as calmly as she could, "please, come quickly. Someone has been hurt...I think dead."

Kent stood by, slightly behind her, waiting as she made the all important call. She continued to speak into her cell phone.

"I'm at Blake Hall, on campus. The experimental computer lab...on the main floor--on the north side, by the parking lot entrance--all the way to the end of the side hallway." She turned her head to Kent and whispered to him, "They're on their way. Stay here."

"Don't worry, Dr. B." he responded, "I'm not going anywhere."

She returned her attention to the cell phone as she heard the voice ask additional questions.

"Yes, this is Dr. Barnes, Pamela Barnes. I'm in the Psychology Department. I just found her...Dr. Clark...here...in the lab." She looked over at Charlotte. "Please, hurry!" she urged into the cell phone. Then she listened as the voice at the other end was evidently giving her instructions.

"Okay, just a minute." She handed the cell phone to Kent. "Hold this and stay on the line," she said to him. Then she carefully bent over Charlotte Clark and placed her hand firmly on Charlotte's neck, feeling for a pulse. There was none. After a few seconds, she then gingerly bent down close to Charlotte's face to listen for breath noises. Charlotte's head was turned to the left, her mouth open. Pamela placed her ear close to Charlotte's mouth. All she sensed was the smell of cigarette smoke—Charlotte was a habitual smoker. It was quite obvious to Pamela that there was no breath coming from Charlotte Clark's body. She was dead.

She then stood up and stepped back from the body, her eyes never leaving the corpse. As she held her hand out to Kent, he placed the cell phone back in it.

"I just checked for pulse and breathing sounds," she told the police dispatcher on the phone. "I couldn't feel or hear anything." She continued listening to the voice and the obvious directions that were being given. "No," she answered into the phone, "Don't worry. I won't touch anything. Yes, I'll stay right here." She turned her head to Kent and whispered to him, "Kent, please go to the outside entrance and direct the campus police here when they arrive. It should be any minute now."

"Right, Dr. B," he said, hurrying out the lab door, "I'm on my way!"

With Kent's departure, Pamela was alone. As she stared down at the body of Charlotte Clark, it suddenly dawned on her exactly what she was seeing. This was not a natural death. Charlotte didn't keel over from a sudden heart attack. The power cord wrapped around her neck made it perfectly clear that Charlotte had been murdered. Oh, my God, she thought. Here they were worried about lab security because of the fear of theft. No one had even considered the possibility that anyone was actually in physical danger when they were alone in the lab. The lab was Charlotte's domain--her pride and joy. It was her efforts that had secured the funding for the lab. She spent many hours here. To think that she would actually die in the place of her glory. It was horrible.

Poor Charlotte. No, thought Pamela, Charlotte wasn't one of her favorite persons. She was abrasive and confrontational, but Pamela had never personally suffered any of Charlotte's verbal attacks—as Mitchell had earlier this evening. Oh, my God, what had happened here tonight?

As she stood there looking at Charlotte and contemplating all of the possibilities, she could hear Kent's voice and the voices of several other people--probably the police--coming down the hallway. Kent entered the lab, followed by medical personnel and two uniformed officers who quickly took over. She and Kent stood back, out of the way. The officers told them to wait because the local detectives would want to question them when they arrived.

She and Kent edged to the back of the lab and sat in two carrels in the last row of computers where they waited for at least twenty minutes. The lab was cold—to protect the equipment—and well lit, much better lit than the rest of the old building. Pamela found herself shivering; she wasn't sure if it was from the cold or her own fear. Finally, the local police arrived and added to the crazy scene. Eventually, a tall man in a shabby grey suit and overcoat strode over to them and introduced himself. Pamela and Kent rose to greet him.

"Ms. Barnes?" he said, holding out his hand, "I'm Detective Shoop." She shook his hand perfunctorily. "Ms. Barnes," said Shoop, "were you the one who discovered the body?" He had a droopy sad face with lids that hung over his eyes like wrinkled prunes.

"No, my graduate assistant Kent Drummond, here, did," she said.

"All right." The detective motioned for them to be seated again as he pulled out a chair for himself from one of the carrels, and the threesome gathered in a circle at the back of the lab. "Let's talk about the details of all of this a bit," he said.

Pamela and Kent sat close together on their lab chairs. Pamela was clutching her jacket and purse and Kent was still holding tightly to his backpack. Shoop straddled the small rolling lab chair from behind.

"Now, start at the beginning," said the tall detective, leaning over the back of the chair and sleepily eyeing the two of them.

"We'd just finished Dr. Barnes' seminar," stated Kent. He glanced at Pamela.

"When was that?" interrupted Shoop.

"About five to nine," answered Pamela, "I checked my watch as I was leaving the seminar room."

"Good," nodded Shoop, then he pointed to Kent, indicating that he should continue. Shoop reached in his suit pocket and pulled out a large cloth handkerchief and wiped his nose firmly. Then he replaced the hanky in his pocket.

"Uh, Dr. Barnes wanted me to check to see if the lab was locked, so I came down here to check."

"Is this laboratory typically left unlocked?" Shoop asked, directing this comment to Pamela.

"No, never," she responded firmly. "There is so much expensive equipment here. Only faculty members have keys, and graduate students can check out keys only with a faculty member's permission."

"Hmmm," said Shoop, thinking and biting his lower lip. "Continue."

"When I got here," said Kent, "the door was open..."

"Open?" asked Shoop, "Is that normal?"

Kent thought a moment. "Not for this time of night, no. That's what struck me as odd right away. I mean, it's usually closed and locked when the last grad assistant leaves for the day. Hardly anyone uses it this late. I figured that a faculty member must be in the lab working late and when I saw Dr. Clark, that's what I thought it was--until I saw how she was..."

"Yes," said Shoop, cutting him off. "Then what did you do?"

"I ran back to the seminar room to get Dr. Barnes," he responded.

"Did you see anyone in the lab? Or near the lab, either before or after you first entered at nine o'clock?" Shoop asked the young man.

"No. No one," replied Kent. "The building was deserted except for Dr. Barnes and me."

Another man in a suit and overcoat arrived and waved a greeting to Detective Shoop, who pointed him towards the body.

"The coroner," announced Shoop. He redirected his interest back to Pamela and Kent. "Now, Mr. Drummond, did you or Ms. Barnes touch the body or anything around the body or in the lab after you entered?"

"No," said Kent, "I didn't touch anything."

"I touched Charlotte," responded Pamela. "I checked her pulse and listened for breath sounds. The police operator directed me to do that."

"Yes," nodded Shoop, "yes, that's fine. Did you touch anything else?"

"No, nothing." she responded.

"All right," Shoop said, standing. "Mr. Drummond, I'm going to have you go with Officer Kline, here." He motioned for one of the uniformed officers to come over. "He'll ask you some more questions, standard procedure, and then he'll see that you're returned safely to your residence." The uniformed officer escorted Kent out of the laboratory. Pamela remained seated.

"Now, Ms. Barnes," began the lanky detective, looking around. "Is there some place more private we could talk?"

"Tonight?" she asked. "Couldn't this wait until tomorrow? I'm so tired. So drained emotionally. I really need to go home."

"I understand, Ms. Barnes," said the detective, "But, I'm sorry. I must ask you some questions right now, while all of this is still fresh in your mind." He looked at her expectantly.

"I guess we can go to my office," she said, sighing, "It's upstairs."

"Fine," he responded and started to lead her out of the lab, his dark overcoat flapping against his legs as he walked.

"Detective," she said, stopping him, hesitating, "Could I first please call my husband? He's probably worried that I'm not home yet."

"Sure," stated Shoop, returning to his chair and reseating himself, obviously intending to wait for her while she made her call. Pamela again reached into her purse and pulled out her cell phone. She pressed the number key for her home. Her husband answered almost immediately.

"Hey, Babe," he said, "Where are you?"

"Oh, Rocky," she said, tears now welling up, "I...I ...won't be home for a while. There was an...an accident here." Then she added quickly, sensing his concern, "I'm fine. I'm fine, but...one of our faculty has died. The police are here. I'm going to be here a bit longer."

"Do you need me to come get you?" he asked. She could hear his voice catch.

"No," she said, gulping. "I'm really fine. I just need to talk to the police a bit more. I'll explain everything when I get home. Oh, Rocky..."

"Yes, Babe?"

"Please, wait up."

"You know it."

She hung up and slowly put her phone away. Then as Detective Shoop gestured for her to lead the way to her office, she headed out of the lab, with a quick final look toward the carrel that contained the body of Charlotte Clark.

Chapter 3

She couldn't believe she was still here--still in the building this late at night. She placed her key in the lock and opened her office. Shoop immediately brushed past her, reached for the light switch, which he found instinctively to the left of the door. Bright stark fluorescent light illuminated her usually cheerful space. Shoop strode to her paisley sofa, removed his overcoat, and laid it over the arm. Then he sat perfunctorily in the middle. He gestured for her to take a place at her desk.

"Have a seat, Ms. Barnes," he motioned, pulling his small notebook and pen from his shirt pocket. She moved to her desk, dumped her belongings on top and sat in her swivel chair. Usually she preferred to lounge on the sofa.   It was more comfortable and she had discovered over the years that if she allowed students to take up a position on her couch, they had a tendency to stay there for a long time. Please don't let this be the case with Shoop, she prayed. She desperately wanted to go home to Rocky. She needed to feel his arms around her and hear him tell her this was all a bad dream.

Shoop crossed one leg over the other and leaned back in the soft pillows of her sofa. He looked entrenched. Not what she wanted.

"All right, Ms. Barnes," he started, flipping through the pages of the notebook and glancing at the notes he'd taken in the lab. "Let's start at the beginning. When did you arrive here?"

"You mean tonight?" she asked, somewhat confused.

"Yes," he answered. "You weren't here all day?"

"No, sir," she said. She was sitting up straight in her desk chair, not feeling one bit relaxed. She knew she had nothing to hide and yet this was quickly beginning to feel like an interrogation.

"When did you first arrive at the building today?" he asked, rephrasing his question, and poising his pen for her response.

"I got here this morning around nine o'clock, but I went home for dinner about five o'clock and then returned at six," she described.

"Is this your regular daily pattern?" he asked, now munching thoughtfully on the end of the pen, his sleepy brown eyes watching her, as he glanced over the tops of his rimless glasses.

"No," she said, swallowing, "only on Tuesdays. I have a graduate seminar on Tuesday nights."

"I see," he nodded. "Hmm," he added, changing positions. "All right, take me again through every step from the time you entered the building at six."

"All right," she said. "I parked in the lot. One of my students, Kent Drummond, you know, you met him ..."

"Right," he cut her off. He pulled his handkerchief from his pocket and wiped his nose. "Continue with your story."

She suddenly felt defensive. "It's not a story," she said. "I'm just telling you what actually happened."

"Right, right," he said in a practiced soothing voice, "Just continue." He shoved the hanky back in his pocket.

"Kent met me at my car."

"Where did he come from? The building?" asked Shoop.

"No, I believe he'd just arrived. His car was parked behind mine."

"Fine," answered the detective. "Go on."

We walked into the building together," Pamela continued, "He went directly to the seminar room and I stopped at the main office."

"Did anyone see you in the office?"

"I was just going to say, I stopped at the office because Phineas Ottenback, one of my colleagues, wanted to talk to me. I stood in the hallway for just a few minutes talking to Phineas and then he headed upstairs to his class and I went into the office to get my mail."

"Where did this Phineas Ottenback come from?" said Shoop, holding up his hand to slow her down, "Did you see?"

"At first, from the main office. But, originally, I suppose, he came from his office. That's at the other end of the hall."

"Near the lab?" he asked.

"Yes, near the lab. Several faculty members have offices in the side hallway that ends at the lab."

"Who?" he asked.

"Let's see," she answered, "Rex Tyson is on the left as you face the lab, the graduate students' office is on the right, Phin's office is next to Rex's. Then Charlotte's office is at the end of the hall, directly opposite the lab. Laura Delmondo's office is next to Charlotte's. Dr. Marks's office--he's the head of our department--is off the departmental office which is directly opposite the main entrance to the building."

"Are those the only faculty offices on the main floor?"

"They're the only ones in this wing. There are two other offices in the other wing of the building--the animal wing. Bob Goodman and Arliss MacGregor teach all the animal psychology classes and their offices are located in that wing."

"And your office is here on the second floor," he said. "Are there any other faculty offices up here?"

"Yes," Pamela answered, "Just Dr. Bentley's which is directly across the hall from mine and Dr. Swinton's which is next to Dr. Bentley's."

"Other than this Dr. Ottenback," he noted, jotting down this information in his notebook, "did you notice any other faculty members in the building tonight?"

"Yes," she answered. "Dr. Marks was in his office talking to Charlotte, but I just heard them, I didn't really see them."

"You're sure you heard the victim, Charlotte Clark in Dr. Marks' office?"

"Yes," answered Pamela, "and I heard her leave and walk down the hall shortly after I entered my classroom." She looked down at her hands folded in her lap. Just how much of what she'd heard between Mitchell and Charlotte should she reveal?

"Did Dr. Marks remain in his office or did he also leave?"

"As far as I know, he remained, although I don't know for sure, because I started class almost immediately and when class was over, I went immediately to the lab when Kent called me."

"Yes," said Shoop. "I see." He jotted away in his small notebook.

Now," said Shoop, his droopy eye lids crinkling, "back to your activities following your arrival at the building tonight. After you spoke to. . ." he trailed away, checking his notes, "Ottenback and overheard the conversation between Marks and Clark, then what did you do?"

"Do?" she questioned. "As I told you, I went to my class, spent three hours teaching, and then a few minutes before nine I dismissed class. I asked Kent--he's my assistant, so he's used to running errands for me--I asked him to run down to the lab and make sure it was locked."

"Why did you do that?" he queried. "Was there some reason you feared that it wouldn't be locked?"

"No," Pamela hesitated, "but we've been warned lately from upper administration and from Dr. Marks to be ultra careful about lab security. The lab contains some extremely expensive equipment and it wouldn't take much for someone to steal it if the door was left unlocked."

"Who, again, has keys?" Shoop asked.

"Every faculty member has a key of their own. I assume Jane Marie, the departmental secretary, has a key--or at least access to one," she pondered. "A graduate student can check out a key when they're conducting their own research or aiding a faculty member with research."

"So, how many keys to the lab, would you say, are out there?" he asked directly.

She thought, counting faculty, Jane Marie, and adding an extra few for graduate students. "I would guess that there are probably 15 or 20."

"But you don't know for sure?"

"No," she answered, "But Dr. Marks, the head of the department, could tell you that."

"And I'll be talking to him, you can be assured," noted Shoop. "Now, Ms. Barnes, please continue with your stor--your description of events."

"I asked Kent to run down to check on the lab to be sure it was locked.," she said, "He did and as I was heading towards the exit, he came running toward me, horribly upset. I followed him to the lab and that's where we found Charlotte."

Shoop bent forward on the sofa, looking at her pointedly.

"Tell me precisely what you saw from the moment you entered the lab."

"The door was open, as Kent told you. He went in and went straight to Computer Carrel #4 and I followed. As I rounded the first row of computers I could see a woman seated in the carrel, bent over the computer desk. I could see the glare from the computer screen so I assumed the person was working at the computer."

"You say 'Computer Carrel #4,'" he stopped her. "Did you know the number of the carrel before you got there?"

"Yes, actually. All the carrels in the first row are numbered. The computers in the first row have more technological features than those in the other rows. The department has subscriptions to several expensive online data bases, and faculty and graduate students can tap into those from any of the computers in the first row. Also, there are sophisticated recording capabilities in each of the first row computers--sensitive microphones and recording paraphernalia that don't exist on the other computers."

"You mean," Shoop asked, "the computers in the first row can do things that the other computers can't?

"Right," she said, smiling, now more in her area. "They can do things even our office computers can't do. That's why you'll often find faculty working on the computers in the first row."

"Did Charlotte Clark use these first row computers a lot?" he asked.

"I'd assume she did; it was her lab," Pamela said, almost laughing.

"Her lab?" he asked.

"I mean, she shared it, but it was through her efforts and fame that we even had the lab," she said. "So, yes, Detective, in a way, it was her lab."

"But, did you see her there, yourself, a lot?"

"No," Pamela answered, "our schedules didn't cross much. I believe she tended to work at night. I usually do most of my lab work during the day."

Shoop readjusted his position. He obviously was striving to become more comfortable. He pulled his large handkerchief from his pocket again and blew his nose, then rolled the cloth up tight and returned it to his pocket. Pamela sensed she was in for a much longer grilling.

"Now, Ms. Barnes," he continued, "You say, Dr. Clark considered the lab her lab. Did anyone to your knowledge resent this?"

Pamela laughed out loud at this.   "Detective," she said, shaking her head, "You have to understand academics. They resent everything--particularly their colleagues who are more successful. Charlotte is—was--absolutely the most successful faculty member in this department, in, I would venture to say, the college, maybe even the University. She'd been interviewed on *Oprah* and the *Today* show. Her research was well-funded; some famous pharmaceutical companies were backing her research on drug addiction. She was the authority on teenage drug addiction--addiction of any sort. She made this department what it is. So, yes, there was resentment, but what you have to understand, is that there was also gratitude, because without Charlotte Clark, we wouldn't have this amazing laboratory, and Charlotte was nothing if she wasn't generous in allowing--no-- encouraging her colleagues to make use of it.   She even discussed outfitting the lab with each of us before it was built. She asked us what sort of features we each wanted in the lab for our own research before it was funded. I couldn't do the type of research I do in the way I do it if it weren't for Charlotte."

"Yes," he said. "A wonderful benefactress. But someone killed her, Ms. Barnes. And it appears--at least from a cursory observation--that nothing was stolen, so why would anyone go into the lab, kill Charlotte Clark, and not take one piece of all that expensive equipment?"

"I don't know," answered Pamela. "I just don't know."

"Is it possible," he prompted, "that someone wanted her dead?"

"I ... I ...suppose," stammered Pamela.

"Can you think of anyone who might want that, Ms. Barnes?" he asked, snorting up another sniffle.

"I can think of many people who were annoyed with her or resented her, but ---wanted her dead----no," she said, "I simply don't believe that anyone..."

"Anyone in your department at least," he filled in.

"Why would it have to be someone in our department?" she asked. "I mean, maybe she went into the lab, left the door open, and someone came in and killed her."

"Some stranger who didn't know her or have any relationship with her, just happens in, strangles her to death, and leaves without taking anything," he said, his shaggy eye brows punctuating his point.

"It does sound unlikely," said Pamela, weakly.

"Tell me, Ms. Barnes," he mused suddenly, "would Charlotte Clark—or any faculty member, for that matter—be likely to work in this expensive lab alone late at night—with the door wide open? Given your security concerns, is that likely? Or would it be more likely that she would lock herself in?"

"Hmm," said Pamela, "It's hard to say. Charlotte is no shrinking violet, but she is very protective of the lab. I'd say she'd keep it locked when she was working late."

"And yet," he noted, "when your assistant discovered her body, he says the lab door was open and the lights were on. If Dr. Clark was working in a locked lab, as you imagine she was, the killer would have had to have a key to gain entrance, no?"

"I guess," responded Pamela, "I just can't imagine Charlotte working alone in the lab that late with the door wide open. It would just be inviting trouble."

"I think I've got enough for now, Ms. Barnes," Shoop said, suddenly, closing his notebook and sticking it back in his shirt pocket. "Should I have one of the detectives drive you home?"

"No," she answered, "I'd really rather drive myself. I'll need my car tomorrow."

"Fine," he noted, rising, grabbing his overcoat, and heading towards the door. "I'll be downstairs in the lab, probably for several more hours, while the Crime Scene folks collect evidence. If you change your mind, just come by. I'll want to talk to you again, I'm sure." He handed her his card. "If you think of anything--or anybody--that you didn't mention, please give me a call." He turned and loped down the hall.

Pamela stood and watched him go. Then she sank back into her desk chair, shaking her head. This did not look good for the department—not at all.

Chapter 4

Pamela left her office and exited the building as quickly as she could. The Blake Hall parking lot was lit up like an airport runway. Several police vehicles, the coroner's van, and other cars were parked helter-skelter, with their various lights blazing and blinking. Pamela almost ran to her car, covering her panting sounds as she quickly unlocked her door and jumped inside. It was hard to shut the door because of the wind, but she finally managed to get inside and start the motor--her fingers trembling badly. She carefully maneuvered her Civic into reverse and out of the small lot, being careful not to speed—not something easy for her. Wanting to get home as fast as she could, she still didn't want to do anything that would jeopardize her safety or cause her to risk breaking a law--however minor. She already had a few moving violations and tonight was not the time to acquire another.

She drove slowly down the winding campus streets she knew so well. The old brick buildings with white wood trim, the towering white columns and the enormous elms and oaks, interspersed with magnolia and cypress always made the campus feel like a page from Civil War history. Here and there the streets and the sidewalks were cracked from years of wear and the many hurricanes whose remnants had managed to blow far enough north to reach their small town of Reardon. She passed the library—closed now after 11:00 p.m.—the largest structure on campus, right in the center of campus, with sidewalks jutting out from it at all angles, going to all the various different buildings that surrounded it. Although much of the campus was in disrepair, it still maintained its old Southern charm, Pamela thought, sort of the Blanche DuBois of the academic world. It was a deceptive look, however, because Grace University was a renowned research university which offered doctorates in five areas—although not in Psychology, her field, which offered Masters' degrees only.

As she left the campus grounds and headed onto Jackson Drive, Reardon's main street, she noticed at once that there was hardly any traffic--not unusual for this late on a Tuesday night. Very few cars were on the streets. The whole place had a ghostly appearance—unlike the Blake Hall parking lot she had just left. She was not accustomed to driving this late at night. Her night vision was not good and she just didn't like driving at night--and alone--this night especially. With clear roads ahead, however, she picked up speed.

As she passed Reardon's downtown area, neon signs from some businesses twinkled on either side of the street. One side street, she knew, wound around behind the city square where the famous Reardon Coffee Factory was located. The Coffee Factory was actually a misnomer, because Romulus Reardon, the town's founder, had established the business during the Civil War to produce coffee substitutes for the Confederate troops when real coffee became impossible to import due to Union blockades. His efforts had been so successful that his line of alternative coffee products made from beets, sweet potatoes, and other local produce now brought tourists from around the globe to the charming factory/restaurant. However, at this time of night, the Reardon Coffee Factory would have few patrons.

Other than a few cars on Jackson, she saw no signs of life. Life, she thought--the life that had been snuffed out tonight. The life of someone she knew. And she'd seen the results personally. She couldn't help but replay the events of the preceding hours in her mind as she drove. Her foot pressed harder on the gas pedal and she drove instinctively.

She couldn't stop the picture from forming in her mind. The picture of Charlotte--her body slumped over in the computer carrel, head lying askance, arms hanging loosely, and that power cord from the headphones wrapped sinuously like a giant snake around her neck. It was so gruesome. Charlotte's eyes open, her skin just starting to turn a color Pamela couldn't and wouldn't want to describe.

Suddenly she arrived at—almost ran through one of the dozen or so stoplights on her route. Hitting her brakes hard, her car reverberated from the effort. Sitting all alone at the light made her more frightened, even though her car doors were locked. She had a nagging sense that someone--maybe the murderer— no, that was ridiculous--but someone might leap out and force her to open the car door. The light changed to green and she breathed audibly. She thought suddenly, "If I hadn't sent Kent back to check on the lab being locked for the night, he wouldn't have found Charlotte and I wouldn't have discovered her and called the police. I'd be home now, in bed asleep. Someone else would have discovered her body--probably tomorrow."

She drove past her dog's veterinarian, a friendly man who always made her smile and whom her poodle Candide genuinely seemed to enjoy visiting. Not so, "visiting" with Detective Shoop. Now there was someone who was all business. He seemed to have little concern for the trauma that she and Kent were experiencing and was only interested in wrenching as much information as he could from her before he felt compelled to excuse her. She knew he'd be back tomorrow and more interrogation would occur. If only she hadn't found the body. That meant more questioning.

Now she was past the inhabited part of Reardon and headed out into the "boonies" where her house was located. The speed limit here was 50 and Pamela increased hers several miles an hour over that. She thought back to when she had arrived at the building tonight. Why couldn't she remember? Were any of her colleagues there? She'd told Shoop that she didn't see any faculty members in their offices—other than talking to Phineas and hearing Mitchell and Charlotte argue in Mitchell's office. Was she right about that? Obviously, Phineas was there because she'd spoken to him. Oh, my God, could Phineas have finished his class early and gone down to the lab and found Charlotte there and killed her? He seemed all concerned about the Tenure Committee when she'd spoken to him earlier and Charlotte was the Chair of that committee. Maybe Charlotte threatened to prevent him from getting tenure. Surely, that wasn't possible.

Or could Mitchell have chased Charlotte down the hall after their fight, followed her into the lab and killed her? Charlotte had certainly reamed him out during that argument. What could they have been fighting about? It might have been something that Mitchell simply couldn't stand and he felt obligated to do something about it—something like kill Charlotte. Oh, that was ridiculous.

Of course, the person who killed Charlotte could have been someone from outside--someone they didn't know, maybe someone who wanted to steal some of the equipment in the lab. After all, that's why Mitchell was so paranoid about lab security. He obviously felt that the equipment in it was threatened. Well, Pamela thought, maybe Mitchell was right. Maybe, someone waited for Charlotte to open the lab, went in, strangled her, and then...stole something? Stole what? If something major had been taken, Pamela hadn't noticed. She supposed the thief could have taken some small items, but, for God's sake, why murder someone for petty theft? It was driving her crazy.

Driving. Yes, driving. Just concentrate on driving. She was whizzing past fields now going around 70. This was the quieter part of her drive; she preferred this segment usually, but not tonight. It was too dark, too quiet. What if her car broke down out here? She started pondering again the events of the night. What had she seen when she entered the lab? What exactly did Charlotte look like? Charlotte was seated in Carrel #4, Pamela remembered. Was the computer screen on? Yes, she was sure of it. That meant that Charlotte must have been working on the computer, probably using the subscriber databases. What was she researching? Why would Charlotte have this horrendous fight with Mitchell and then run to the lab to do research? Did her computer research have something to do with Mitchell and their fight? That's ridiculous. She was probably just working on her addiction research. Pamela tried to remember what Charlotte was working on—what was on the computer screen. She simply couldn't picture it and it was too late now to find out because Charlotte's body had probably been removed and the police had no doubt checked the computer for evidence and turned it off. Oh, Charlotte was probably just doing her addiction research. For Pamela, it was hard enough keeping track of her own research much less remember what studies all her colleagues were doing too. It was unlikely that Charlotte was collecting her own data. She was probably doing some sort of background research for one of her projects. That would be why she was in the lab and not working in her office; she needed information from the online subscription databases. She tried to remember what was on the screen when she had found Charlotte's body.

Now on Pamela's right was *All America* gym--where her daughter had studied gymnastics for many years when she was younger. Those were easier, happier days when Angie was in grade school; there was so much more drama now that Angie was a teenager. A few more blocks and she'd be home. Rocky would be there waiting for her. What would she say to him? When she'd called him earlier, she'd only told him that someone had died and that she'd be late. He must be crazy with worry. Oh, God, please, give her strength to get through this.

A rabbit--no, a squirrel--bounded across the narrow road onto which she'd just turned off Jackson Drive. Pamela slammed the brakes suddenly. Her car screeched to a halt and her body lurched forward, straining at her seat belt. She paused a moment to catch her breath, then carefully, ever so carefully, started back on her way. There was much less light on these narrow residential streets and the last thing she wanted to do was hit something--like a family pet or—worse--a person.

She thought back to Charlotte, slumped over. That power cord, dangling. The computer screen was lit up brightly, she was sure. What else? What else was Charlotte doing? Surely she wasn't recording; that wasn't something Charlotte typically did even though she could have recorded from the carrel she was in. And what did it matter what she was doing, thought Pamela. Why does what she was doing necessarily have anything to do with her murder? If the killer was a thief, he could have followed her into the lab and Charlotte was just in the way.

No, reasoned Pamela. She wasn't just in the way. If that were the case, we'd surely have found her body in the doorway, as if she were trying to prevent someone from entering or leaving, possibly. The fact that she was seated and had been strangled from behind, said to Pamela--and it said it to her quite suddenly--that Charlotte was murdered intentionally and the killer had sneaked up on her from behind. There was no confrontation. Charlotte didn't realize the killer was there until that power cord tightened around her neck.

Oh, my God, Pamela thought. Somebody intended to kill Charlotte Clark. She felt sure of it. She didn't know why it didn't dawn on her when she first saw Charlotte's body there in the lab, but now that she thought about it, there was no other possibility. Maybe.

She turned onto Colonial Court, her street, her headlights leading the way to her house which was about halfway down the lane. Each house she knew like a member of her family. Charlotte had no immediate family that Pamela knew of. The only people Charlotte really knew were her colleagues in the Department--the only people who could be considered on a list of possible suspects. And if the animosity Mitchell probably felt towards Charlotte after experiencing her wrath earlier this evening was shared by other faculty members, then the list of suspects could include virtually everyone in the Department.

She pushed the garage door opener on her key chain and the door slowly rose. Rocky was standing in the kitchen doorway, lit from behind. With exquisite care, she pulled into the garage, opened the car door, and slid out. Then she rushed towards Rocky's waiting figure.

Chapter 5

Oh, how good his arms felt around her. She wanted to just stand there in his embrace forever, but after a few moments, she pulled back. Rocky was appropriately named. He was a large, burly man, with short brown hair and stubble on his craggy face. He took her books and her purse from her shoulder and set them on the kitchen table. Then he carefully removed her jacket, placing it over the back of the kitchen chair. With his arm tightly around her shoulder, he guided her towards the bedroom.

"Oh, God, Rocky," she cried in a small voice, "It was awful. You just can't imagine."

He sat her down on the edge of their bed and with ritualistic care bent down and removed her heels, placing them neatly to the side. Then, quietly, he brought her a robe and nightgown which were hanging from a hook on the bathroom door.

"Where's Angie?" she asked.

"She wanted to talk to you, but I told her you had to stay late for something. She went to bed hours ago," he said.

"She wanted to talk to me?" she asked.

"Yeah," he said, "Something about a car. Don't ask."

"Did she finish her homework?"

"Early," he said, "Then spent most of the night trying out different hairdos or whatever you women do."

Their daughter was just beginning her college career. She had been a good student in high school—and never engaged in any of the typical adolescent problems such as drinking, drugs, or wild partying. Even so, Angela was a handful and her attitude was often belligerent and morose. She never seemed to fit in and her friends were few.

"Where's Candide?" she wondered, looking around for her usual little greeter.

"Under the bed, asleep, I think. Now," he said, "Quit stalling, soldier. Get those clothes off and into your jams." She obeyed robotically, her eyes staring straight ahead. When she was comfortably clothed, she leaned back on the bed where Rocky had piled some pillows against the headboard.

"I need to talk to you," she said, whispering.

"I know," he said, touching her shoulders gently but firmly, "Wait just a minute." He went quickly into the kitchen and returned almost immediately with a cup of steaming liquid.

"Hot chocolate with latte foam just like you like," he pronounced softly. "I thought it would help calm and relax you."

She took the steaming cup of warm liquid and sipped it slowly.

"Thank you," she smiled up at him. "You're the best."

He rounded the bed and propped himself up next to her. Rocky had spent most of his life as a career military man—an Army sergeant—a cook to be exact. They had met in graduate school at a new student orientation. Their chemistry had been instant and they had married within a year of meeting. When Pamela had continued on for her doctorate, Rocky had been happy to remain at the instructor level with his Masters' degree and be a house husband, caring for their young daughter. He made good use of both his teaching skills and his military training to mold his students. Pamela always felt secure with him because he approached all crises with calmness and firmness. She knew she would need his fortitude in the coming days.

"Now," he said, looking straight at her. "Tell me what happened."

"I found her," she said, gulping. "I mean, one of my students actually found her, but..."

"Wait a minute, Babe," he interrupted. "You'd better start at the beginning. All I know is that someone died and you had to stay late."

"Right," she nodded. "It was Charlotte. Charlotte Clark."

"You mean the diva?" he asked.

"Yes," she answered, "I mean, she was famous, Rocky. She'd just been on *Oprah*, for God's sake."

"Did she have a heart attack?"

"My God, no!" she sat up abruptly. "She was murdered!"

"What?" he exclaimed.

"That's what I meant. I found her," she repeated. "I found her body."

"What makes you think she was murdered?" he asked, a patch of wrinkle lines appearing over his nose. "Did you see someone kill her?"

"No," she responded, "But when Kent found her--he's my graduate assistant--he called me to the lab, and I went there and I saw her. She had a power cord from a set of headphones wrapped around her neck."

"God," he exhaled. His face contorted into a frown. "You were there by yourself?"

"No," she said. "Kent was there."

"But, the two of you were alone in the building?" he asked, developing that slow burn that she recognized as a prelude to his very infrequent outbursts.

"It was after nine and all the evening classes were over. Everyone was out of the building as far as I knew."

"Except the person who killed Charlotte," he said.

"We didn't see anyone at all," she responded. She could see how worried he was for her.

"What did you do then?" he asked, calming some what.

"We called the campus police and they came almost at once," she said. "That's why I was there so late. Then the local police-- this Detective Shoop was asking me questions until just a little bit ago."

"Couldn't he have waited until tomorrow?" he queried, now more annoyed than angry. She'd finished her chocolate. He took her cup and placed it on his nightstand.

"Rocky," she said, feeling much too tired to get into an argument with him over her safety, "It's all right. I'm home. The police wanted to get my reactions while they were fresh in my mind. I understand. Everything turned out all right." She looked at him and put her hands on his face as if to say, "I'm safe." She loved this dear, sweet man who had her best interests at the very top of his list.

Rocky gave in to her plea and stood up long enough to draw back the covers on their bed. She snuggled inside the warm bed. Rocky climbed in beside her and turned out the light.

"I don't think I can sleep," she said, her shoulders quivering.

"I didn't expect you would," he responded. "Just try to relax. This has been a terrible ordeal for you. You should stay home tomorrow."

"No," she muttered, "I can't do that. It'll be a zoo over there. Things will be in an uproar and the students will be upset. I have to be there. And besides, that Shoop will probably want to question me again."

"Pammie, Babe," he said, nuzzling close to her ear and wrapping his arms around her in the way that always made her feel totally safe and secure, "You don't need to feel obligated to go in. My God, you found a dead body tonight. Anyone would understand if you wanted to take the day off tomorrow."

"I'll be fine," she said, turning towards him. "Right now, my brain's on overdrive. I can't stop thinking about it."

"I can imagine," he responded. "It must have been horrible-- finding a dead body." They whispered, nose to nose.

"Yes, it was creepy," she said, "I mean, I've seen dead bodies at funerals, but never like this. And I had to touch her--you know--to check her pulse and listen for breath sounds. That was scary. The very thought of it gives me the willies."

"You were never one to tolerate blood well," he said, flashing her a half smile. "Wasn't it third grade when your classmates got some sort of shot and you fainted?"

"And I didn't even get the shot," she answered, "I'm a wimp." She stuck out her lower lip.

"You proved your bravery tonight," he said, squeezing her.

"There was no bravery involved," she said. "It was just odd. I keep thinking about it, wondering what happened. I mean, did some stranger come into the lab while Charlotte was sitting there, and for no reason strangle her?"

"Is that what the police think happened?" he asked.

"They don't say exactly. I mean, Detective Shoop didn't really say what he thought," she noted. "He just asked what I'd seen and what I knew."

"And?" he suggested.

"I keep thinking about it and it doesn't make any sense."

"What doesn't?" he asked.

"Why would some stranger go into a lab, kill someone sitting there at a computer terminal, and then leave without taking anything?"

"They didn't take anything?" he asked. "I thought that lab of yours was full of expensive equipment."

"It is," she said. "That's why it's so strange. If it was a killing tied to a theft, then why didn't the thief take something? I know that lab like the back of my hand, Rocky, and I'd swear that nothing--at least nothing of value--was missing."

Pamela couldn't see her husband's face but she could feel his breath on her cheek. She could feel his body tense as his brain tried to process this information.

"Then why?" he asked.

"I think the person wanted to kill Charlotte," she said. There was a long pause as Rocky pondered her words.

"Why?" he asked finally.

"I don't know," she answered.

"But you could be in danger," he said, "The entire faculty could be."

"I don't think so," she said, "I mean, it's unlikely. Some crazed person trying to wipe out the entire Psychology Department?"

"Stranger things have happened, he added.

"Rocky," she scolded, "Remember you teach English literature. You have a far more vivid imagination than I do. I evaluate everything scientifically."

"Oh, yes," he nuzzled her nose, "I know how scientific you are, Miss 'I-don't need to read the recipe, I'll just put in a little bit of this and a little bit of that.'"

Rocky was an excellent cook and a stickler for following recipes to the letter. She laughed. Then, suddenly, she stopped.

"Oh, God," she said, "here I am laughing and one of my colleagues has been murdered."

"Life goes on, Babe," he said.

"Yes," she answered, "But, I was there. I'm in the thick of this whether I want to be or not. Someone murdered Charlotte and more than likely it was intentional. It's also more than likely that it's someone I know."

"Such as who--?" he paused, curious and worried at once.

"I don't have the slightest idea," she mused. "If I go by who disliked Charlotte it could be anyone. I mean, she antagonized just about everyone in the Department. Just before my class tonight I overheard her in a huge fight with our department head, Mitchell Marks, right in his office. I had just gone into my classroom when Charlotte stormed out of his office in a huff. And on top of that, Charlotte is--was the Chair of the Tenure Committee and three of our faculty members are up for tenure. At the last faculty meeting, I recall, she demanded that all the tenure candidates include their doctoral dissertations in their tenure portfolios. Can you imagine that?"

"She didn't really expect all the committee members to read three dissertations, did she?   That'd be like reading three novels—three long, boring novels."

"I don't know. They're sitting in her office as far as I know. I sure haven't had time to read any of them. I guess I figured I'd go down and thumb through them just to see what they were about. But it wouldn't matter what we committee members did or didn't do. Charlotte pretty much controlled who would and who wouldn't get tenure."

"Yeah," he nodded, yawning. "That would make for enemies. But surely not for murder. I'm glad I'm just an instructor and don't have to worry about tenure."

"It's a ridiculously outdated system, isn't it? Oh, who knows why she was murdered? We may never know." She scooted down in the bed. "I've got to get some sleep. What time is it anyway? No, no. Don't tell me."

"Your wish," he answered, yawning again. She rolled over and fluffed her pillow. The silence in the room was haunting. Then she heard the soft, delicate little snuffles of their poodle Candide, snoring lightly under the bed, his favorite sleeping place.

There were so many questions, so many details that were just starting to come into focus about the death of Charlotte Clark. Pamela had found the body and thus, she felt a sense of obligation to find some answers to those questions. But they'd have to wait. They'd have to wait until tomorrow and, for all she knew, that was only a few hours away.

Chapter 6

When Pamela arrived at work the next morning, it was just before nine o'clock. As she came through the Blake Hall parking lot entrance, she could see that the police had draped yellow "crime scene" tape over the lab door, barring any entrance. As far as she could tell, all faculty office doors were closed. As she walked towards the main office, she passed Charlotte's office. That too, had yellow tape covering it. She wondered why, as no crime had occurred there. She assumed that the police had or would be examining Charlotte's computer and personal items in her office and wanted to keep people out of there.

As she walked down the hallway, she didn't see any of her colleagues. Either none of them had arrived yet or they'd already heard about Charlotte's death and were lying low. When she entered the main office, she spied Jane Marie Mira, the departmental secretary, typing at her keyboard, but obviously keeping an eye on Mitchell Marks' office door which was closed. Jane Marie had been with the department for as long as Pamela had been there. She was a highly competent and fiercely loyal watch dog of their Chair, and actually, the entire faculty. Pamela quietly made herself known to Jane Marie and gestured to her.

"He's with the police," Jane Marie whispered, "Oh, Dr. Barnes, you poor thing! Finding Dr. Clark like that. You must have been horrified!" She came out from behind her desk festooned with Halloween decorations and a Jack-o-lantern full of candies and hugged Pamela. The softness of her cashmere sweater felt good against Pamela's face.

"It was unpleasant," Pamela said to her friend and co-worker, "It makes me cringe just thinking about it. When did Mitchell find out?"

"He said the police called him at home last night," Jane Marie replied, "They called the Dean too. All upper administration knows. It'll be all over the news today. Didn't you hear them talking about it on the local radio?"

"No," responded Pamela, "I try to keep things quiet when I'm driving. I, uh, have trouble concentrating on the road, sometimes. Do you know who's in there with Mitchell?"

"Some tall guy. Snoop? Or Scoop?" Jane Marie said.

"Shoop," corrected Pamela.

"That's it," Jane Marie said. "He's a weird bird."

"Tell me," agreed Pamela, "He was questioning me in my office--afterwards--last night until at least eleven."

"Oh, God," said Jane Marie, "Why didn't you call in sick this morning?"

"That's what Rocky said to do," Pamela responded, "But I figured I'd better meet my classes. They're going to be upset-- even more so when it gets out that I found the body."

"Listen, Dr. Barnes," continued Jane Marie, "If you change your mind, just let me know. I'll see that your classes are cancelled. You might feel a lot better if you just went home. I mean, the police are probably going to want to talk to you again, aren't they?"

"Yes," Pamela answered, sighing. "Shoop made that clear. That's actually another reason I felt I needed to be here. If he asks for me, tell him I'm in class until noon and then I'll be in my office."

"Okay," said Jane Marie, shaking her head of pretty brown curls, "but I really think you should get out of here." She shook her finger at Pamela.

"I appreciate your concern," said Pamela, "but I'm going to tough it out."

Jane Marie bit her lower lip and looked down. Pamela sensed a problem.

"What's wrong?" she asked.

"Dr. Barnes, don't tell anyone, but there was an envelope in Dr. Marks' mailbox this morning when I arrived that wasn't there when I left last night."

"Maybe a faculty member left it for him. I was in the office last night after you locked up and I'm sure other faculty were too."

"Did you see anyone?"

"Phineas was just leaving as I was going in and...well...Charlotte was in Mitchell's office. They appeared to be having quite a fight."

The young secretary blanched. "A fight? With Dr. Clark?" She scowled and leaned back in her chair. "That's what I was afraid of."

"Why? What's wrong?"

"I took the envelope out of his mailbox this morning and I opened it. I suspected that Dr. Clark was the one who put it in his mailbox. It looked like her private stationery."

"What was in it?" Pamela asked, moving closer to Jane Marie's desk.

"I probably shouldn't have opened it, but I am his secretary and I often open his mail. It didn't say 'personal' on it and I might have opened it on a very busy day and even called it to his attention. Now, I almost wish I had called it to his attention so I could see his reaction when I showed it to him," she spewed out her narrative so fast that Pamela could barely follow her.

"But it's too late now," continued Jane Marie, even faster, "He opened it himself. Or, rather I think he opened it himself, so I won't be able to see him react. Maybe he hasn't opened it. It could still be sitting there on his desk unopened. He was horribly upset when he came in. Opening his mail was probably the furthest thing on his mind."

"Jane Marie!" shouted Pamela in a stage whisper, "What was in the envelope?"

"Do you think I'm horrible for opening it? I was just concerned for him? I just want to protect him."

"No, you're not horrible. You have his best interests at heart. What was in the envelope?"

"If I tell you, you have to promise not to tell anyone."

"All right, all right," Pamela nodded. "I won't tell. Just tell me what was in this mysterious envelope that you think Dr. Clark put in Dr. Marks's mailbox."

"It was a photograph of a woman."

"A woman?" Pamela asked. "What woman?" She pulled up a chair next to the secretary's desk.

"I don't know," said Jane Marie. "I'd never seen her before." She rubbed her face again, stroking her cheeks upward as if they were the source of her grief.

"Was it his wife?"

"No, not Velma," said Jane Marie, "I know her. I'd recognize her photograph, even an old one."

"Describe it," ordered Pamela, scooting her chair closer to Jane Marie.

"It was a black and white photo and it appeared to be snipped from a newspaper--fairly recently. The woman looked to be in her mid-thirties. Pretty. Smiling. Blonde. Very stylish."

"Was there anything written on the photograph?"

"No, I checked. Nothing front or back. No handwriting. No print."

"Why would Charlotte put a photograph of a woman no one knows in an envelope and stick it in Mitchell's mailbox?"

"My question exactly," said Jane Marie. "Do you think it has something to do with their fight?"

"Maybe. But I may be wrong in my other assumption."

"What other assumption?" asked Jane Marie.

"That it's a photograph of a woman no one knows. You don't know her, but that doesn't mean that Mitchell doesn't."

"You're right," said Jane Marie, her eyes and mouth widening in concert. "What should we do?"

"Nothing," announced Pamela. She stood up.

"But what if it's related to Dr. Clark's death?" she said, trembling.

"Jane Marie," said Pamela, firmly. "If I were you, I'd forget that you ever saw that photograph. This is Mitchell's problem. He's an adult--and head of the department, I might add. If he believes it's pertinent to Charlotte's death, I'm sure he'll mention it to the police." Jane Marie seemed to take solace from Pamela's words.

"You're right. Thank you, Dr. Barnes. Have a candy." She held out the Jack-o-lantern and Pamela grabbed a wrapped toffee.

"You're welcome." She smiled weakly. After grabbing her mail out of her slot, she started to go, but stopped when another thought crossed her mind. She turned abruptly, frowning.

"What?" asked Jane Marie, "Oh, Dr. Barnes, you do think that photo is related to Dr. Clark's death don't you?"

"I don't know. They did have that fight last night." Pamela stood there scowling.

"I know, but, surely that isn't related to her death." Jane Marie looked at Pamela. "I mean, I thought someone came into the lab and attacked her--someone unknown. That's what Mitchell thought it must be."

"They don't know much yet," answered Pamela, "We'll just have to wait and see." Keeping her eyes on Jane Marie, Pamela turned and headed out of the main office, not looking where she was going.

As she exited, she bumped into a younger colleague, Rex Tyson, entering, looking dapper in a grey pinstripe suit. Rex was Phineas Ottenback's research partner and the two of them made a prolific and productive team. However, they were as different as two professors could be—Phin being the shy, nebbish, and Rex, the dynamic, gregarious ladies' man. Pamela knew that their interests in deviant personality behavior obviously brought them together as researchers, but they were definitely the departmental odd couple—although she doubted they were homosexuals, as both had wives--somewhere. Neither wife appeared with any regularity at department functions.

"My God, Pamela," Rex crooned, "You came to work? I thought for sure you'd stay home. How awful for you to discover Charlotte like that."

"Yes," she agreed, "Not at all pleasant."

"You really shouldn't be here," he reiterated in his warm voice, placing his hands gently under her elbow. "I mean, you really shouldn't have come in." He tsk-tsked her with a sympathetic smile and two very deep dimples.

"Maybe not," she sighed, "but I'm here now, so I'm going to stay." She smiled at him. Really, she wasn't an invalid, she thought, and she wished people would quit acting as if she were. She continued on her way up the side stairs towards her office.

Now, hours later, after her morning classes, she found herself sitting on her sofa eating her lunch. It was a lovely thin-sliced turkey sandwich on a crescent roll--with tomatoes, endive lettuce, and a creamy garlic sauce. Normally, Pamela would be savoring each delectable morsel. But today, she just couldn't enjoy it. Rocky loved being her personal chef and had created her favorite sandwich, knowing how stressful the day would be for her. She sipped her orange spiced tea from the thermos he always packed. He'd even included two crispy Madeleines that he baked last week. She smiled as she thought of the effort her sweet husband invested into creating these sack lunches for her as well as their family dinners. The Army had taught him the basics but he had taken that knowledge to new heights of gourmet magnificence. For her, it would be work, but for him gourmet cooking was therapy—more like an obsession, something like working out at the gym was for her. Oh, my God, it had been ages since she'd worked out and she could feel her thighs expanding just sitting here....

She grabbed her hair brush from her purse and walked to her full-length mirror on the back of her office door (great for checking to see if one's slip was showing before class) so she could run her brush through her hair. She perused her form and face. Every time she saw herself in the mirror, it didn't seem like the person she pictured in her own mind—definitely older, plumper, and not nearly as cheerful-looking as she usually felt. Did she look particularly more stressed today than usual? She couldn't tell. She certainly felt it. Flip, flip. A few strokes with her brush and her hair-do looked renewed.

Replacing her brush in her pocketbook, she returned to her couch and half-heartedly attempted to nibble on her sandwich for a while. Suddenly she stopped mid-bite. Here she was munching away, drifting off, when one of her colleagues had just been murdered. What kind of a person are you? she chided. Then, answering her own question, she responded mentally, Oh, give yourself a break, Pamela. This is the first moment she'd actually sat down and relaxed since she'd arrived on campus this morning.

She had awakened at her regular hour of seven o'clock and had made sure both Rocky and Angela were up and got to their classes on time. As for Rocky, he'd been out the door with only a brief kiss and a whispered warning to be careful. Rocky never let his feelings stand in the way of his duty—part of his military training—and something he'd instilled in both her and Angela over the years.

Her daughter Angela had been petulant, almost as if one of her mother's colleagues dying was a personal affront to her. She had wanted to talk to Pamela the previous night and was upset that her mother had had to stay late. Angela changed her tune, however, when she discovered that her mother had found the dead woman. Then, she'd seemed suddenly intrigued and Pamela had had to provide her with a blow by blow description of what had happened while she prepared Angela's breakfast—not a pleasant combination What a ghastly way to bond with my child, Pamela had thought—crime and cereal. However, the previous night's events had provided them an opportunity for a rare mother-daughter conversation which eventually turned to more mundane matters:

"How did that essay come out that you were working on last night?" Pamela had asked.

"I turned it in," answered her daughter.

"Good," said Pamela, carefully, not wanting to unwittingly tackle a topic that would antagonize Angela during this brief conversation opportunity. "What was it about?"

"I told you. We had to write about some difficult experience we had. I wrote about Carl."

"You did?" questioned Pamela. She was surprised that her daughter had actually discussed the painful experience she'd had with a boy in junior high school who suddenly began bullying her for no valid reason. The boy had terrorized several students, not just Angela, and eventually had been shipped off to boarding school by his parents. The bullying had stopped but the pain had lingered for Angela.

"Did you get your paper back?" asked Pamela.

"Not yet."

She wanted to quiz her daughter further about the content of the essay, but decided that Angela would reveal what she wanted in her own good time. For the moment, Pamela was happy to hear that Angela had managed to face this particular demon in a positive, constructive way and that she was able to discuss it with her mother. She only hoped that the English professor would not belittle Angela's revelations or focus so totally on her vocabulary and grammatical mistakes that Angela would regret writing about the wrenching event. Angela struggled with every aspect of her life. She seemed to look for—or at least expect-- the worst in everything, especially herself. The results of that early bullying experience just wouldn't seem to go away.

Now, sitting here on her office couch, as she thought about their talk this morning, Pamela felt a small tear gather in the corner of her eye. She loved this little girl--or rather this young woman--for Angela was now eighteen and a college freshman, although Pamela often wondered if Angela had the same feelings for her. Even a slight show of affection from her daughter would be appreciated.

Was all that this morning?   It seemed like years ago. Yesterday--last night--the discovery of the body now seemed like it had occurred in another decade. Pamela felt in limbo. It was all she could do just to eat her sandwich—and think.

She wondered if she should ring Jane Marie's extension to see what was going on downstairs. Maybe the police were finished interviewing Mitchell. She'd like to know the outcome. She'd like to know if--when--Shoop would be coming back to talk to her. Surely, he would. If she had more questions in just the few hours since she'd discovered Charlotte's body, surely he would too.

She hadn't mentioned to Shoop that Charlotte and Mitchell had been arguing when she overheard them talking in Mitchell's office last night before the murder. Now there was the issue of the weird photograph that Charlotte had apparently placed in Mitchell's mailbox after the argument. Having never before been interrogated in a murder investigation, she really wasn't sure what was and what was not an appropriate concern for discussion.

She finished her sandwich. It was delicious. As she sipped her spiced tea, she thought back to her classes this morning. Oh, the students had been difficult, as she knew they would be. In the past when tragedy had struck--like 9/11 or Hurricane

Katrina--students needed class time to process the event. The death of Charlotte Clark was no different, except it was closer to home and scarier.

Many of her students had questions about what had happened. Many were concerned for their own safety because they assumed that a murder in the building meant that a possible serial killer was on the loose. Pamela tried her best to allay those fears. She assured them that the police thought (although she was not completely sure what the police thought) that Charlotte Clark's murder was an isolated event. Dr. Clark was alone in the lab, she said, and it was very late at night. If they continued to be reasonably cautious, they needn't be afraid. That seemed to calm them somewhat.

Some students seemed worried about Pamela's welfare also. They expressed concern that she might have been in danger. This touched Pamela deeply, and she admitted to herself that she was frightened, although she tried not to let her students see her fear.

But her fear was not so much that some maniac was on the loose somewhere on campus and might strike at any moment. No, her fear was of something more insidious. Someone had killed Charlotte Clark, and Pamela did not think, any more than Detective Shoop evidently thought, that it was done by a thief caught in the act of stealing equipment from the lab. Pamela was beginning to believe more and more strongly that whoever killed Charlotte had intended to do so for reasons of their own, reasons that had nothing to do with theft.

Chapter 7

She heard the crisp, sharp tapping of footsteps coming quickly towards her office. She recognized the sound of Dr. Joan Bentley's sturdy, yet lady-like heels. Joan appeared at her door, and knocked. Pamela leaned back on her sofa.

"Thank God, it's you," she sighed, looking up at Joan.

"My dear," said Joan, entering and setting herself primly on the straight back chair near the door. "You've been a busy girl since I saw you yesterday. What a horrible night for you!" The older woman tilted her head of white hair, stylishly coiffed in a loose bob, and looked expectantly towards Pamela.

"Joan," Pamela sighed, "When did you hear?"

"Arliss called me last night," Joan said. "We debated whether to call you at home, but decided we'd talk to you today. You needed your sleep."

"Arliss heard about it last night?"

"It was on the local eleven o'clock news," reported Joan calmly, nodding.

"Did they mention me finding her?"

"No, dear," Joan answered, "But they said a female colleague in the Psychology Department who was teaching a night class found her. That would be you."

"No," groaned Pamela. "I don't want to get involved with reporters."

"Just avoid them. If they ask to interview you, just say no," she replied, as if it were quite simple. Pamela wished Joan would loan her the magic wand she used whenever she encountered a nosy reporter. Joan was a well-known researcher in her own area of educational psychology, almost as famous as Charlotte Clark was in the field of addiction. Some of Joan's studies had even drawn attention from the local media and she was well-accustomed to handling the press.

Pamela heard the sound of another set of footsteps heading down the hallway. She recognized this pair also--the long, striding, sneaker-clad gait of Arliss MacGregor. Arliss's head appeared in her doorway. Arliss was lean and lanky and dressed more like a boy, in trousers, a man-shirt, and a vest--than like the instructor and lab director that she was.

"My God, Pam!" She entered the office, waving her arms around. "What happened?" She plopped down in Pamela's desk chair.

"I wish I knew," said Pamela. "I wish I'd just gone home last night instead of checking to see if the lab was locked. Someone else would have found her then."

"Thank you, Mitchell Marks!" announced Arliss, hands on hips, "Protect our computer lab at all costs! Who knows what you may find there?"

"Arliss!" chided Joan, "This has been a traumatic experience for Pamela. Just imagine finding a dead body."

"And to make it worse--it was Charlotte's," said Arliss, pulling a wayward black lock out of her face and back into her ponytail.

"Arliss," said Joan.

"Come on, Joan," sneered Arliss, "You didn't like her any better than anyone else did." She leaned back and put her feet up on the desk. Pamela was not thrilled when Arliss took over her desk like this, but it was one of the drawbacks she tolerated in order to maintain her favored position on her sofa.

"I didn't wish her dead," said Joan, her nostrils puffing out as her nose rose skyward. She folded her hands neatly on her lap.

"Neither did I," said Arliss, slamming her feet firmly on the floor.

"Please, you two!" Pamela cried, throwing her hands up in defense. "Can't we stop this?"

"I'm sorry, Pam," said Arliss, "really, I am. For you, I have nothing but sympathy." She blinked and stuck out her lower lip.

"Yes, dear," agreed Joan, reaching over and patting Pamela's hand. "We both are here for you. You're the one we're concerned about. Nobody can do anything now for Charlotte anyway."

"So," Arliss, began again, "What can we do to help you? Anything. Just ask." She flung her arms wide in a gesture of conciliation.

"Yes, dear, why don't you take a day or two off? I'd be glad to cover your classes." Joan offered, flouncing her skirt out a bit as she edged closer on her chair.

"Me too," agreed Arliss. The two friends edged closer to Pamela, hoping to provide support.

"No," said Pamela, firmly. "That's not what I need. I need to keep busy. My mind is working overtime. I just can't stop thinking about it."

"Oh, my!" exclaimed Joan, shaking her head, "it must have been horrible."

"What did she look like? I mean, was it gross?" asked Arliss, *sotto voce*, scooting even closer to Pamela on Pamela's wheeled desk chair.

"Arliss!" responded Joan, "I can't believe you. You're not typically so insensitive." She gave Arliss a penetrating stare.

"Hey," said Arliss, "I'm just curious. Pam's the first person I've ever known to discover a dead body. Don't pretend that you aren't curious too, Joan." She peered back at Joan over the tops of her black frame glasses.

"Ladies," said Pamela, holding up her hands and calming her two friends as best she could, "I'm happy to share my experience with you. Lord knows, I had no special feeling for Charlotte, but she was a fellow human being, so I'd at least like to be civil, if that's acceptable?"

"Just tell us the juicy details and we'll be models of civility," agreed Arliss, flinging one arm in front of herself in a sweeping gesture. Joan nodded in agreement.

"There's really not much to relate," said Pamela, "Kent Drummond, my graduate assistant, went to check on the security lock in the lab after our seminar, and almost immediately came running back yelling. I went down there and discovered Charlotte, at Carrel #4, bent over, the power cord from a headphone set wrapped around her neck. It was quite obvious she was dead." She related all the events of the previous evening for her two friends, including the gruesome details for Arliss' benefit and concluded with, "That was it. Nothing more."

"Nothing more," said Arliss. "Correct me if I'm wrong, but doesn't a power cord around her neck mean she was murdered?" Arliss whispered this last part.

"Surely not," said Joan, eyes wide.

"I saw it, and it certainly didn't have the appearance of one of those freak accidental power cord strangulation deaths," said Pamela.

"I can't believe that someone would intentionally kill Charlotte," maintained Joan. "Yes, she was an overbearing, obnoxious prima donna, but you don't kill people for that. Besides, we were all beholden to her, financially at least. She had national recognition. She had clout. And that brought in money this department would never have seen if she hadn't been the star that she was."

"Too bad she had to have such an unpleasant personality," noted Arliss.

"Isn't it?" sighed Joan, shaking her head. "I don't know why we can't all behave like professionals and not little children. I mean, we're psychologists; we study behavior. You'd think we'd recognize unpleasant patterns in our own behavior when they occur, that she would have recognized the unpleasant patterns in her behavior."

"At least she wasn't an addict--not that I know of, anyway. She was an expert on addiction," added Pamela.

"She was addicted to cigarettes," noted Arliss.

Pamela and Joan both laughed.

"I suppose she was especially testy lately because of the pressure she was under as Chair of the Tenure Committee," said Joan, with a coy smile.

"Pressure?" asked Pamela.

"From the Dean, to curtail our number of candidates," responded Joan.

"But, Joan," responded Pamela, "I thought she was fighting the Dean on this tenure business. At least, that's the impression I had." That, thought Pamela, was probably what her complaint was about the Dean in her fight with Mitchell last night. "Besides, we can't choose or not choose who goes up for tenure based upon the Dean's request. That's a departmental decision."

"Don't be naive, Pamela," whispered Joan, bending closer to the younger professor, "I've been in this department and on this campus longer than any of you, and I know our Dean. He'll do what he has to do to make ends meet, and if that means limiting tenure candidates—so be it. Besides, why would Charlotte have had any compunction about dropping one or more of the candidates? Well, maybe not Laura; she was her protégé, but certainly not Rex or Phin. It was nothing to her and she might even have used her chairmanship of the committee as a bargaining chip with the Dean."

"You mean, she would have offered to cut one of our tenure candidates from the list if..." Arliss asked.

"Certainly, to get the Dean to do something she wanted, or even to get retribution against Mitchell. He was not her favorite person," noted Joan.

"Joan, I can't believe Charlotte would do something like.... Oh, I just can't stand even thinking about it any more." Pamela sighed audibly and wrapped her arms around herself. The other two women looked at her with concern and then glanced at each other.

"I believe there's only one solution," said Joan, with delight.

"What?" asked Arliss, with anticipation, sitting up straight and turning directly to face her more sophisticated friend.

"A night of riotous drinking at *Who-Who's*," Joan answered.

"Yes," Pamela agreed. "It's been ages since we 'owls' have put our heads together and solved all the world's problems while downing a pitcher of Margaritas."

"I for one," said Arliss, perking up, "could use several pitchers. The situation with the animal lab has me in such an emotional pit that I just can't think straight."

"Arliss, you can't let the animal lab become your personal crusade," said Pamela.

"Yes, dear," added Joan to Pamela's concerned comment, "Make Bob Goodman handle it. He's in charge over there—not you. He needs to solve the financial problems in the animal lab."

"But, Joan, Pam, if he doesn't solve them soon, he'll be gone, and I'll be out of a job," said Arliss, her shoulders sinking in dejection.

"Now, dear," said Joan, "you're young. You have your whole life ahead of you. What about going on for your Ph.D.? Didn't you tell us that was your ultimate goal? If Grace University's animal lab folds, it would be the perfect opportunity for you to strike out on your own."

"But, I don't want the lab folding to be my motivation. I want my motivation to be something positive." Arliss sat with her elbows on her knees looking down at the floor. She shivered. "This lab means so much to me, to Bob; we're doing such important work there. I just don't see why the department can't come up with enough funds to help us maintain it better."

"There, there, dear," said Joan. "I'm sure something will happen soon. You never know what's around the corner." Joan reached over and placed a soothing hand on Arliss' shoulder.

"I say we plan our *Who-Who's* outing for this Friday, ladies," announced Pamela suddenly. "Okay?"

Both women immediately perked up and nodded in agreement. Joan smoothed her flowered dress. Arliss poked her glasses up her nose. Both women seemed to realize at that moment that it was getting late and that they needed to go.

"Well, dears," announced Joan, grabbing her keys from Pamela's desk and standing abruptly. "I must be going. I have that paper for *Educational Psychology Abstracts* that must be finished and off to the editor by tomorrow. It'll be a late night for me." She stepped lively to the door and turned, "Friday it is. *Who-Who's*." Then she was gone.

Arliss remained seated. Pamela looked suspiciously at her friend.

"What is it, Arliss?"

"Joan talking about me going back for my Ph.D. just made me even sadder. I hadn't thought about that in ages." Arliss lifted her head. "Pam, all I can think about is the lab. You just don't know what a mess it is. I'm trying so hard, but we don't even have a graduate assistant. We have over 40 mice and the two chimps, Sheila and Bailey. Bob's making so many advances with Bailey. You wouldn't believe how much progress he's making with the little fellow. Bailey is really recognizing and expressing different human emotions. I mean, Bob's close to a breakthrough. And it all could be jeopardized because of

Charlotte Clark and her stupid million-dollar grants depriving our animal lab from getting even the most meager of maintenance funding. Now that she's dead, there's probably no chance of our lab ever getting any of that funding."

"Arliss," Pamela said, moved to see her friend in such turmoil. "I wish there was something I could do."

"Just listen," replied Arliss. "Just listen." The two friends sat like that for a second or two.

Suddenly, Kent, appeared at the door. He was wearing jeans and his customary black t-shirt, today with a flaming dragon design on the front.

"Hey, Dr. B, I contacted all our experimental participants and cancelled them for today. I figured with the police in the lab, you know, that we couldn't collect data. Do you think I should cancel our subjects for the rest of the week too?" asked the energetic young man.

"Kent, thank you for thinking of that. Yes, cancel all week. Our experiment totally slipped my mind, what with..." stammered Pamela.

"It's okay, Dr. B. I figured you'd be upset after what happened last night," he said softly.

"Kent, this is Miss MacGregor, from the Animal Lab," introduced Pamela. "Arliss, this is Kent Drummond, my grad assistant."

"Hey, Miss MacGregor, I know you. The rat lady—ooops-- no offense," he stammered; his spiky hair edged in purple remained rock solid as if his head had been dipped in glue.

"None taken," answered Arliss, laughing. "You're not the first to call me 'Rat Lady,' Kent."

"I'll touch base with you later, Dr. B!" announced Kent. Pamela waved to him as he disappeared down the hallway.

Pamela heard the sound of two sets of footsteps coming down the hallway. Bob Goodman and Willard Swinton came into view in her doorway.

"Dr. Barnes," greeted Willard with a slight bow. He was a large, rotund African-American man, dressed nattily in a brown suit with an orange shirt and matching bow tie. He was leaning on an ivory-handled cane. "Dr. Goodman and I thought we should come and see how you're doing," he said, his buttery voice sonorous enough to be doing food commercials. Willard was a departmental fixture, his warm, courtly demeanor always upbeat, even though his physical health seemed to be deteriorating more and more each year. His smiling face belied the pain he obviously felt with every slow step he took. Pamela and Willard shared research interests in linguistics and often conferred on various research problems.

"Yes, Pam," agreed Bob Goodman, a tall, slim, even emaciated, man, his hands embedded tightly in the pockets of his jacket, "We heard about your ordeal on the news and from Jane Marie. My God, what a terrible thing for you, for the department, for all of us." Pamela was surprised to see Bob on her side of the building. He was typically ensconced in his animal lab or teaching one of the several courses the department offered in animal psychology. She kept up with his activities mostly from reports from Arliss, who, as his laboratory director, worked closely with him.

"Absolutely," intoned Willard, "Absolutely terrible for all of us." His bow tie wobbled as he spoke. Pamela looked around at the small crowd that was beginning to form in her office. She had nothing against popularity. In fact, she liked being popular, but she surely didn't want to acquire popularity by finding dead bodies--particularly the dead bodies of her colleagues.

"Thank you, everyone, really," she sighed, "But, truly, what I need is...."

Just then, the phone rang. She stood up and went to her desk to answer it. After listening for a brief period, she groaned, placed her hand over the receiver, and spoke to the entire group, "It's Jane Marie. Mitchell's called an emergency faculty meeting for tomorrow morning at seven a.m.!"

Arliss threw up her arms and spun around on Pamela's desk chair. Willard sighed and leaned more heavily on his cane. Bob groaned.

Pamela turned back to the phone. She heard Jane Marie then inform her that Detective Shoop was on his way up to her office. He had a few more questions for her.

"Wonderful," she replied, "Can this day get any better?"

Chapter 8

She didn't know how it happened but Shoop was again seated in her office, his lanky body draped over the back of her sofa. He had greeted her colleagues officially and then requested some private time for additional questioning "if she didn't mind." Of course not, she thought, I love being grilled about a murdered colleague by the police. I love recalling every ugly moment of finding Charlotte's body in the lab.

She was seated on her desk chair, no longer in her comfortable spot on her sofa. She felt robbed. This big giant of a man was not only invading her privacy, he was invading her space. She steeled herself for the onslaught of questions.

"Now, Dr. Barnes," noted Shoop, as he pulled out his trusty black notebook.

At least he's using my title today, thought Pamela.

"Let's go over your testimony from yesterday." His lack of enthusiasm radiated from his droopy eye lids to his slumped posture.

Testimony, she thought. He makes it sound as if I'm in court. I'm not certain if anything I said yesterday is accurate. I was so distraught, she thought. She put her hand to her head and rested her elbow on her desk.

"I know that it's hard to think back," he started. Out came the handkerchief. Pamela tried to avoid cringing.

"Detective," she interrupted, "To be frank, thinking back is all I can do. I can't get any of it out of my mind. I'd like a break from it for just a brief moment, but no one will let me do that." She contorted her face and rubbed her eyes.

"I'm truly sorry, ma'am," he said, reaching for a tissue from a container at the edge of her desk and handing it to her.

"No, no," she said, brushing it away, thinking of the germs transferring from his large hanky to her tissue. "I'm fine, really. Let's just get on with it. What else do you need to know?"

"Dr. Barnes," he said, "You say that you can think of nothing else.   While you're thinking...have you remembered any information that you didn't mention when we spoke yesterday? I mean, you were traumatized. You'd just discovered a colleague, murdered. You undoubtedly were upset and not thinking clearly. Now, after a passage of time, you might remember things that you didn't yesterday."

"Detective," she said simply, "To be frank, I don't remember what I said to you yesterday."

"Let me review the highlights of your testimony," he replied, opening his notebook. At this, he quickly ran through several pages of his notes, very thorough ones, she observed.

"All right, all right," she said, thinking. "One thing I did remember was the computer screen--it was on."

And that was strange to you?" he asked.

"Not strange," she said, "But it did suggest why Charlotte was in the lab. The computers in the first row are equipped with special subscription databases that we don't have available on our office computers. I believe I mentioned that."

"And you think," he completed her thought, "that Dr. Clark was probably in the lab using this subscription service?"

"I would say it was likely," answered Pamela. "Charlotte visited the lab often to check on research studies of hers being conducted there, but there were no subjects or graduate assistants there last night, which I know because my assistant Kent checked the lab sign-up sheet and my experiment was the only one scheduled in the lab this week and there was no one scheduled to be working in the lab last night because he was in class—with me. So, I can only assume Charlotte was there to use the databases."

"All right," he said, jotting this information in his notebook. "Is there any other reason Dr. Clark might have been in the lab late at night at that carrel?"

"It would be unlikely," responded Pamela, "that she'd be recording. Her uses of the lab tend toward survey data collection for her studies on addiction. She's world famous, you know."

"So I keep hearing," he said, reaching again for his hanky and letting loose another blow. He replaced the hanky in his pocket and Pamela breathed in relief. "Would the computer screen be on if Dr. Clark were recording?"

"Not necessarily," said Pamela, "You can record directly by using the toggle switch on the computer desk. However, if you want to keep a copy of what you record, you'd have the screen on and a file selected. I didn't see anything like that, so I doubt she was recording."

Shoop paused and stared at her a bit, then scribbled a few notes in his small pad. Then he asked, "So, would there be anything else she might have been doing there in the lab in that first row of computers?"

"No," said Pamela firmly, "she'd either be using the databases or recording. If she wanted to do anything else, such as general Internet research or writing, there'd be no reason to do it in the lab. She could use her office computer."

"Good," he noted. "Assuming she was using this special database service, what sorts of things might she be doing with that information?"

Pamela rolled her eyes and said, "Detective, I'd have no idea what sort of topic Dr. Clark was investigating--if she was-- probably something to do with addiction. If you really must know, you can probably contact the subscription services—Dr. Marks can give you their contact information--and they could track it down. But, anyway, I just don't see how knowing what she was researching would help find who killed her."

"Dr. Barnes," he said, staring at her intently, his shaggy brows lowered, "It may not have anything to do with her murder, but we're investigating all possibilities. We're working on the assumption that this was not a random killing. We believe--and I am guessing you might be too--given you have 'thought about nothing else,' that Dr. Clark was not the victim of a random crime. We believe, at least at the moment, that someone sought her out and intentionally murdered her."

Pamela cringed. Yes, she'd thought that. But to have Shoop say it formally was frightening for Pamela.

"Just because there was no evidence of theft in the lab?" she asked.

"That," he responded, "and other things. For one, the killer didn't appear to be looking for anything. Apparently, the killer went directly to Dr. Clark and strangled her. Also, there is the fact that the killer picked a time when Dr. Clark was alone, a time when it would be unlikely that anyone else would be around and the killing could be accomplished without witnesses. This murder has all the hallmarks of an intentional crime, Dr. Barnes. That's why I'm back here talking to you. I want you to dig deep into your memory and pull out anything you remember, either from the events that took place when you discovered the body or any other occurrence that might--even in the slightest way--relate to this crime." He leaned forward and spoke in a conspiratorial voice, "Because, Dr. Barnes, this is a murder. There is a killer out there and we don't know who he--or she--is."

"You don't suspect me, do you?" she asked, suddenly flustered.

"No, not at the moment," he responded, "But for the moment, you--and your young assistant--are our only sources of concrete information. We really need your help."

"Are you telling me, Detective Shoop," she phrased her words carefully, "that you believe Charlotte's killer is someone in our department?"

"It's quite possible, Dr. Barnes," he replied, "and until we're certain otherwise, I'd advise you to be very careful who you talk to and what you say. As the person who discovered the body, you may have special knowledge that may lead us to the killer-- even if you don't realize it. The killer may perceive you as a threat and your life could be in danger. I don't say this to scare you, Dr. Barnes, but only to urge you to be cautious in what you say and do. If the killer is one of your colleagues or a staff member or a student, you might inadvertently reveal information which the killer might consider threatening and thus jeopardize your own welfare."

"I couldn't believe that...," she stammered, but the detective continued.

"I noticed," he said, speaking softly but intently, "when I came in that there was a group of your colleagues here chatting. Now, I'm sure they were all just very concerned about you, and their presence gave you a sense of support, but, Dr. Barnes, you don't know who you can trust. So, for the moment, until we catch this person, I'd advise you to keep conversations with people on campus to a minimum--or at least--avoid discussing the murder."

She absorbed this information and the policeman's suggestions. It was difficult to believe that she was in any danger--particularly from her friends and co-workers. Even so, she vowed to do as the man requested.

"All right, Detective," she nodded, "if you think that's best, I'll be very discreet."

"Good," he said, smiling his sad smile and looking over his notebook, which he finally closed and placed back in his shirt pocket. He pushed himself out of the sofa where he'd almost taken root in the soft cushions.

"Detective," she stopped him as he started for the door, "One question."

He turned to her. "I was wondering," she asked, "if your men are still working in the lab? This may sound callous, but I have data collection scheduled in there and I know you have the lab screened off. I was just wondering when we--I mean--the faculty could get back into the lab to work?"

"They're not there now," he said. "But we're leaving the tape up because we may want to get back in. Also we need to go over the lab with your Department Head, Dr. Marks, with his inventory list and confirm that nothing of value is missing. You'll have your lab back in a day or two."

"Thank you, Detective," she said.

He was at the door. He turned back to her. "Oh, and Dr. Barnes, I'm serious. Keep a low profile," he said, "and if you think of something else that might have anything--anything at all to do with Dr. Clark's death-- contact me at once." Then he loped down the hall and out of her sight.

Pamela waited for his disappearance. She looked at her watch; it was after three o'clock. Other than her colleagues earlier and Shoop's visit, no students had shown up for her office hours. That was typical, she noted. Some days it was barren and other days her office was like a zoo. Today's lack of student visitors must be a reaction to Charlotte's murder. She guessed that she too would find it hard to think about academic pursuits if one of her instructors had been murdered.

She glanced out her window at the parking lot below. Shoop was climbing into his car and heading out of the lot. The police still had the lab barricaded, he'd said, but no one was in there now. Reardon was a small town with a small town police department—not the New York City Crime Unit. Just how sophisticated could Reardon's little police department be and what could they possibly have found?

No time like the present, she thought. Quickly, she grabbed her jacket and purse and headed out her office door, locking it securely as she left. As she walked down the hall, she noticed that Joan's and Willard's offices were closed. They were either in class or had left for the day. Hopefully, the situation would be the same on the main floor. As she headed down the stairs, she felt her heart start to beat faster. At the bottom of the steps, she opened the stairwell doors and peeked through. The coast was clear; she could see no one in the side hallway that led to the lab. Quickly she slipped through the doors and down the hall. Shoop was right. The yellow tape was visible at eye level, barring the lab door. The door was securely locked, too, forcing her to fumble in her purse for her keys. As she unlocked the door, stooping carefully under the tape, and went inside, she thought, what are you doing? This is probably exactly what Charlotte did yesterday, and look where it got her.

She looked around the lab. She noted the sign plastered above the check-in table. It's large font stated, "Only graduate students and faculty are allowed keys to this laboratory. Please do not leave the lab unattended."

At the far end of the room were some storage compartments where they kept replacement parts for the computers, microphones, and headphones. She walked to the back of the room and surveyed the entire laboratory.

Taking up almost the entire room were four rows of computer carrels, each with a computer terminal. The second through fourth rows had computer terminals only. The carrels in the first row had computer terminals, free-standing microphones, headphones, and control panels immediately to the right of the free-standing microphones. The front-row booths were all separated by acoustic paneling that rose to a height of eight feet and extended out a width of five feet on both sides.

Pamela walked up the side of the lab and down the first row of carrels. When she arrived at Carrel #4, where the murder had occurred, she saw that the police had removed the computer terminal, keyboard, and microphone, and all the attaching wires. They were probably looking for trace evidence and dusting for fingerprints. She noticed bits of black powder on the interior walls of the carrel and realized that it was probably remnants of fingerprint powder from where the technicians had examined the interior of the booth—its desk, the walls, and probably the chair and the surrounding floor too.

She sat at an unoccupied booth in the first row. Thus seated, she could see no one and hear no one in either booth beside her if anyone were sitting there. She loved these first row terminals. In addition to the extra recording paraphernalia, the computers in the first row also provided the subscription database services that were not available free over the Internet and that had made her research much easier.

Directly in front of her and facing the four rows of computer carrels, was the master control panel. This long table allowed graduate students and faculty to have access to and control of the data being recorded or listened to in any of the 40 carrels. Indicator lights showed which computers were in use. These lights also indicated which computers were in "record" versus "listen" mode. They indicated the number of subjects who had used each terminal each day and how many times each stimulus tape had been played, among other types of data. From the master control panel, a faculty member or graduate assistant could, technically, control anything going on in any of the terminals, and could record--or delete--anything recorded in any terminal.

Carefully, she touched the keyboard in front of her. She noted the various buttons for volume control and other output. The toggle switch, as she had described to Shoop, was located on the right side of the keyboard, slightly toward the front edge of the desk. She imagined Charlotte sitting here. This booth was just like Carrrel #4. Someone had grabbed her from behind and strangled her. Was it at all feasible that Charlotte might have inadvertently bumped or pushed the toggle switch while she was being strangled? If that had happened, Pamela knew that nothing would show on the monitor because Charlotte wasn't attempting to record anything. The police obviously had checked or would check the monitor from Carrel #4 to discover whether or not a recording had been made. But, Pamela reasoned, if Charlotte had bumped the toggle switch and then maybe bumped it back---quite possible if there was a violent struggle---then the sounds of that struggle might have been recorded. Not here on the computer in Carrel #4, but....

She walked directly to the front of the room, toward the master control console and pressed the master power switch. Lights lit up the entire unit. Each terminal was listed by number. On the right side of the console, she found the storage unit, which she knew was the device that kept all recordings made in each carrel in the first row of computers. These recordings were stored until a faculty member or graduate assistant went through and manually deleted them.

As she clicked on the storage unit, the carrels from #1-#10 lit up, each showing a graph for amount of sound recorded. All ten graphs were at zero--except for Carrel # 4, the carrel where Charlotte was found. Oh my God!, she thought. She noted the date--October 30—yesterday! She carefully clicked on the segment. There was only a small amount, probably just a few seconds worth of sound. The time stamp said "8:27 p.m."

She glanced around. Already she'd been here too long. The police techs might return at any moment, and after what Shoop had said to her, she didn't want to run into anyone in here. Grabbing a blank CD from a bottom drawer in the master console, she slid it into the CD slot and hit *duplicate*. The console whizzed and whirled and then quickly stopped. She opened the drawer and removed the CD, placing it back in its paper sleeve and into her purse. Then, after shutting down the console, she gave the lab a quick once over, and when she was certain it was the same as it was when she entered, she hurried out, stopping briefly to duck under the police tape and lock the door behind her.

Chapter 9

She had barely exited the lab and locked the door when she bumped into Rex and Phineas walking out of Rex's office. The two men had obviously been arguing, but they quieted immediately and turned their attention to her.

"Pamela," greeted Rex, warmly, "Surely, you weren't in the lab? I thought the police had forbidden us to enter." He came towards her, followed by Phineas.

"I just had to check on some data," she mumbled, "I'm running an experiment this week and I need to see where we stand on participants. I didn't think they'd mind." She stopped herself before she babbled on unnecessarily.

"Dr. Barnes," said Phineas, coming closer, "I'm so sorry about what happened. I heard you were the one who found Charlotte in the lab. I wish I'd stayed later last night so I could've been here for you."

"Yes," she nodded at the two men, "That would have been nice." She was starting to go.

"So, what did you find?" asked Rex in a low whispered voice, glancing back at the lab door.

"What?" stammered Pamela, clutching her purse as if it contained gold.

"The lab. Did the police make a mess of it? I assume they probably turned the place upside down," boomed Rex, shaking his head of thick chestnut-colored hair.

"Yes," agreed Phineas, nodding fiercely. "Did they--you know--clean everything up?" He grimaced squeamishly.

"It looks as it always did," offered Pamela. "Feel free to go check for yourselves if you like." She was feeling more and more uncomfortable standing here; the newly burned CD felt warm inside her purse.

"Well, take care, Pamela," said Rex, squeezing her arm, "Personally, I believe I'll wait until the police give their approval before I venture into the lab." He had an uncharacteristically somber look on his face.

She stopped suddenly. "Well, that's very circumspect of you, Rex."

"All I meant was," he replied, "that I'd feel uncomfortable to go in there now." Then he smiled that broad, toothy grin.

"Yes," agreed Phineas, nodding insistently. "I wouldn't want to go in the lab unless I absolutely had to. I can just imagine how terrible it must make you must feel, Dr. Barnes. Just being in the lab probably reminds you of Charlotte, of finding her last night. I just can't believe I was here in the building when it happened." He cringed and his mouth gathered into a little pucker.

"Gentlemen," announced Pamela, straightening herself, "I'm perfectly fine and it doesn't bother me to be in the lab. I'm truly sorry about Charlotte, but I'm not going to let what happened to her prevent me from doing my job, and I assume you won't either." She beamed her most gracious smile at them, turned, and headed down the hall toward the main office.

For almost an instant, Pamela forgot the CD in her purse--the disk with seconds, maybe even minutes of sound that had been recorded at the computer desk where Charlotte had been murdered at a time when the murder probably took place. Pamela was anxious to listen to the CD, but she knew that this would be something she'd have to do in private.

She turned the corner toward the main office. Charlotte's office door was closed and the yellow crime scene tape barred all entrance. The main hallway looked reasonably normal once again. The dim lighting in the hallway was interspersed with the warm glow from large hanging lantern chandeliers and matching wall sconces. The sounds of student voices rang from a side hall. As she passed the door to Laura Delmondo's office, she could see Laura sitting at her desk, her head in her hands. The young professor appeared frozen in this position except for some slight heaves from her thin shoulders. Pamela thought how much she wanted to leave work and get home to listen to the CD in her purse, but the sight of a fellow teacher sitting there so forlornly, touched her heart, so she stopped at the doorway and knocked gently.

"Laura," she said softly.

The young woman raised her head and blinked.   "Oh, Pamela," she said, wiping her eyes with the back of her hand, "I'm sorry. I shouldn't be sitting here like this. Students could come in at any moment; it's just that..." She heaved a huge sigh, clutching the side of her head again. Pamela quietly entered the office and shut the door.

"It's okay," she said, sitting on a chair opposite Laura's desk. "This has hit all of us. You're allowed to be upset."

"I know," Laura replied, "I feel so terrible. Charlotte and I had a big fight yesterday. It was the last conversation between us and now she's...she's dead. The last thing I said to her was so hateful."   This was news, thought Pamela.   More than just Mitchell had had a fight with Charlotte yesterday.

"Now, Laura," said Pamela, soothingly, placing her hand on Laura's arm from across the desk, "you and Charlotte were close. I'm sure she knew that you cared for her." Laura's desktop featured a color photograph of Laura and her husband in their wedding attire.

"She knew," said Laura, biting her lower lip, her long golden hair falling around her shoulders in dishevelment. "She knew how much I appreciated her and everything she'd done for me. I mean, I wouldn't be here without Charlotte; she was my mentor. If it hadn't been for her, I never would have considered an academic career or gone on for my doctorate.   She was instrumental in my getting the position here at Grace University too.   I just can't believe she's gone."   Another bout of tears welled up and Laura reached for a handful of tissues from a box on her desk.

"Charlotte cared about you, Laura," said Pamela.   "She showed that by her actions.   She was just a very— argumentative—person, and yesterday you were on the receiving end. It didn't mean she didn't realize your concern for her."

"I did. I did," stammered the younger woman. "She was concerned, but just about my job--always about the job, and my research, and getting published. Pamela, you're a woman--you're married with a child. You know there's more to life than just your job."

"Absolutely, I do," said Pamela, smiling.

"But Charlotte didn't," insisted Laura. "She was all about work. I guess it was because she didn't have a family. She turned me into her family--sort of like her daughter. I thought at first that might be nice because I'm estranged from my own mother and I'd like to have an 'adopted mother,' but Charlotte didn't want me like most mothers would want a daughter. She wanted me as her protégé--and for that I had to produce. Research! Papers! Whatever I published, it was never enough for Charlotte; she was always demanding more."

"She was hard on you just as she was hard on herself," agreed Pamela. "Without a doubt, she was the most prolific researcher I've ever known. And those grants! How could one person produce so much grant money single-handed, I'll never know."

"Me neither," said Laura, "And she expected everyone to be just like her. But, Pamela, no one can do that and have a life. I have a husband and we—we've been wanting to start a family. We haven't been successful and we were just starting to try *in vitro* fertilization."

"I see," nodded Pamela.

"It's very expensive," she confided, "And it's very time-consuming. I simply haven't had any time for working on my research or even for regular classes. I've missed some of my office hours because of all these doctor appointments lately. And Charlotte was harassing me about it to make matters worse. She told me the *in vitro* was all a waste of time and that I needed to forget about being a baby machine."

"Being a baby machine?" asked Pamela delicately.

"Yes," replied Laura, sighing, "Those were her exact words."

Pamela patted Laura's arm again. "It sounds like the insensitive thing Charlotte would say. I feel such sympathy for you."

"Thank you, Pamela," Laura said, smiling demurely. "It really helps to be able to discuss this. I don't have anyone to talk to now that Charlotte is...."

"Listen to me, Laura," Pamela added firmly, "You're better off confiding your personal problems, if you feel the need to do so, to someone—anyone--who'll be more empathetic than Charlotte ever could be."

"Yes, I see that," said Laura, wiping a final tear aside and smiling a much broader grin now.

"Will you be okay?" asked Pamela.

"Yes, thank you," added Laura, "thank you for stopping to talk to me. I really appreciate it." Pamela squeezed Laura's hands with hers, smiling back and then rose to go. She turned at the door.

"Good luck with the *in vitro*," she whispered. "I have tremendous faith in modern science." Then she was off down the hall. She'd forgotten, for the brief duration of her conversation with Laura Delmondo, her original goal. Now, she was doubly motivated to get home.

She pushed through a crowd of students and turned into the main office, quickly grabbing her mail from her slot, and then glanced around the corner into Jane Marie's smaller office. Jane Marie was typing furiously, a ray of sunlight from an outside window piercing through orange and black crepe paper bunting and striking her hair.

"Is he in?" she whispered to Jane Marie, pointing at the Department Head's door.

"Dr. Bentley's in there now," answered Jane Marie, looking up. "She's been in there for at least 20 minutes. He's been looking for you."

"Oh, no," Pamela scowled, "since when?"

"Just a bit ago," she assured Pamela. "He spent most of the morning with that Shoop, and then with the Dean trying to deal with the fall-out from Charlotte's murder, and then this afternoon that woman reporter from local KRDN was here interviewing him and ...."

"He didn't tell her that I was the one who discovered the body, did he?" Pamela asked.

"I don't think so," she said. "I really think they're trying to keep this low key and keep your name and the name of the grad assistant...."

"Kent."

"Yes, Kent. Keep both of your names out of it. But, Dr. Barnes, I wouldn't count on that working. That reporter's a barracuda. She was trying to finagle information from me."

"And?"

"And, of course, she didn't get any," announced Jane Marie, smiling coyly, faking polishing her nails on her chest.

"Thanks."

"No problem," said Jane Marie.

Just then, the door to the Department Head's office opened and Mitchell Marks and Joan Bentley entered the small ante-chamber.

"Pamela!" called out Marks, spying her. "Good, you're here. Can you come in for a moment?"

"I was--," she stammered, desperately hoping to be on her way.

"Don't worry, my dear," tossed out Joan, "He's under duress but he won't bite you. I promise." She stepped lively out of the office and on her way.

"For a moment, then," said Pamela, looking back at Joan, disappearing around the corner, and at Jane Marie, who smiled sheepishly and sorrowfully at the same time.

Mitchell held open the door to his office and escorted Pamela into the vast space, decorated in antique guns, hunting trophies and awards from Mitchell's many years of publishing articles and books in psychology. Her Department Head was tall, medium built, and could, in some circles, be considered attractive, with his wavy blonde hair, blue eyes, and delicate features. A former faculty member had once compared him to the Ashley Wilkes character in "Gone With the Wind." Unfortunately, thought Pamela, Wilkes was ineffectual—as Mitchell often was—at least in his inability to stand up to Charlotte. Pamela found Mitchell's type too effete and far preferred a more macho man—like her Rocky.

"My God," Mitchell sighed, leaning back in his comfortable desk chair. Pamela seated herself on one of the three or four chairs situated in front of his desk. "What a disaster! And here I haven't even had a second to talk to you. I wish you'd called me last night." Mitchell always spoke in a deep whispered monotone. No wonder he had trouble leading the department.

"Mitchell," she started to apologize, "The detectives were interrogating me so long, I didn't have a free second. When I finally got home it was so late and...."

"Stop! Stop!" he said, holding up his hand, "It's not a criticism. I can only imagine how terrible the whole thing was for you. I just wish I'd been here to help you. That's what I meant. No one should have to go through such an ordeal alone." Mitchell leaned way back in his leather desk chair and formed a tent of his fingers. He rocked his chair slowly back and forth as he looked at her with cloudy blue eyes that hid—what? Did he know more than he had revealed about the murder?

"Thank you, Mitchell," she said. "Actually, it's over now. The sooner things get back to normal, the better."

"It's certainly not over," he said, harrumphing and crossing his legs, "The cops will be on this until they find who did it. The press will be plastered all over everyone in the department. Listen, I tried to keep your name out of it and so did the Dean. But I can't guarantee that some clever reporter won't tumble to the fact that you were the one who discovered the body. You're news, Pamela, and reporters will want to talk to you. I've already spoken to Kent and told him in no uncertain terms not to discuss this with anyone except the police if he values his assistantship."

"Mitchell, I don't think we can require that of him," she said, quizzically. "I mean, if he wishes to talk to the press, he's a free agent."

"You're probably right," he sighed, "but I tried. I just hope the police find the culprit sooner rather than later and we can go about our business."

She relaxed noticeably. Mitchell certainly didn't seem to be acting guilty. If he was the one who had murdered Charlotte, he didn't act like it. Or he could just be a good actor. Mitchell had never seen particularly hypocritical to her; he was, in fact, usually very straightforward.

"Do they have any suspects?" she asked, carefully. "I mean, Jane Marie said you'd spoken to the police this afternoon."

"Right," he said, "That big, tall fellow. With the eyebrows. Shoop. Didn't get the feeling that they had any clues, but maybe that's just their way."

Now that she was here, talking to her boss, she figured she might as well test the waters. "It doesn't seem it was a thief or anyone from the outside, I understand," she ventured. "They seem to think it was someone--local."

"Local." He smirked, his eyelids suddenly lifting, shoulders becoming concave. "You mean someone in the department."

"Yes," she agreed, keeping her eyes firmly glued to his.

"Ten faculty members, fifteen graduate students, one secretary, and a few custodians," he said, in a calculated manner. "A fairly small pool."

"Yes," she answered. "But surely not everyone in the pool would have a motive."

"Hmmph," snorted Mitchell, leaning back in his chair again and gnawing a pencil. "Motive to kill the most obnoxious, overbearing, self-centered person I've ever known." He removed the pencil and twirled it between his fingers. "Seems to me like the entire pool would have a motive." He clenched his teeth, and suddenly broke the pencil in half. "Well, I hope you're ready for a damn interesting faculty meeting tomorrow!"

Chapter 10

She couldn't get his words out of her mind. Mitchell's words. He'd said that every one in the department had a motive to murder Charlotte. That was extreme, she knew, but the ramifications of her department head thinking such a thing were staggering. If the police didn't find the killer soon, the investigation would expand, and all of them would be implicated. She couldn't help but be worried. Mitchell had been in the building before the murder and he'd argued with Charlotte. Phineas was also in the building. Laura had fought with Charlotte recently. How many other colleagues could feasibly be listed as possible suspects? Of course, she and Kent were probably considered suspects, she realized, because we were the ones who'd found Charlotte's body.

Pamela thought of the CD she'd made and that was still tucked safely in her purse, even now, on Wednesday evening, as she lounged in her favorite chair in her bedroom, reading student papers and listening to soothing music on cable television. Although she was incredibly anxious to listen to the CD, she knew she didn't dare open it now. Rocky and Angela were in other rooms. She'd have to use the family computer in the study and, even though they probably would ignore her, she couldn't be sure that one or both of them wouldn't ask what she was working on. She just didn't feel she could comfortably lie her way out of that situation.

Candide, her poodle, rubbed against her leg and she reached down and petted his head. He was the only one in the house with whom she could share this secret.

"Hey there, little fellow," she whispered. "Are you as anxious to check out that CD as I am?" Candide sniffed and rolled over on his back, begging for a tummy rub. Pamela obliged, bored with what had turned into several hours of paper grading.

Angela was ensconced at the front door handing out candy to trick-or-treaters. She'd actually volunteered for the job and Rocky was willing to let her have the position seeing as how she'd completed her homework. Every once in a while, Pamela heard the doorbell and Angela's squeals when she recognized the outfits of the tiny costumed children. Rocky had, as usual, prepared a warm, comforting dinner—cornbread and a savory beef and wine concoction he called "Sergeant's Stew." He was now seated at the dining room table grading essays for his freshman English classes. Every once in a while he'd saunter into the bedroom and announce how many papers he'd completed, a sort of contest they had when they were both grading.

She tried to concentrate on the paper she was correcting. She glanced at the various red marks she'd made, hoping to refresh her mind as to the content of the manuscript, with no luck. Oh, she thought, it's no use. I simply won't be able to accomplish anything until I see what—if anything--is on that disk. At that moment, Rocky walked in, with his stack of papers and a gleeful look.

"Done!" he chirped.

"What? No!" she responded, "I was ahead of you just a bit ago."

"You're not keeping up, Babe," he announced. "How many more?" He gestured to the stack of uncorrected papers piled on the hassock in front of her.

"At least forty," she sighed. Rocky always won these grading battles because he didn't agonize over every error the student made. He circled problem areas, made a general assessment, gave a grade, wrote a note of encouragement, and then went on to the next paper. The sooner he finished a stack of papers, the sooner he could be whipping up some new recipe.

"How's Angie doing?," she asked, "Has she run out of treats yet?"

"Nope," he said, "We still have several bags."

She placed the paper she was correcting down, along with her pencil and stretched her arms up in the air. "I can't believe she volunteered to hand out Halloween candy. That's so unlike her. So altruistic."

"She's a college freshman," he mused, "she should take on some adult responsibilities."

"And handing out Halloween candy is what you'd consider an adult responsibility," she laughed at him, poking him in the belly as he moved closer to her, "Maybe next we can have her help us pay off the mortgage."

"Or your traffic tickets." He sat on the edge of the hassock, careful not to disturb her stack of student masterpieces.

"Rocky."

"Sorry. I didn't really get a chance to ask you how things went today," he said softly, putting his large hands on her knees. "Was it hard for you? I hope they were supportive over there. I know that department of yours can be a bunch of pit bulls sometimes."

"Actually," she said, smiling at him, "people were very nice. The students, of course, were concerned too."

"So concerned that they probably thought the best thing for you was to cancel class, right?"

"How well you know them," she laughed.

"I have the same ones, remember," he said.

"I know."

"What about Marks, your Chair?" he queried, "He ought to give you an all-expense paid sabbatical. You deserve it."

"Only," she said, caressing his cheek, "if you can get your Chair to give you one at the same time so we can go away together."

"Ummm," he sighed, snuggling into her neck, "if only." Angela bounded into the room, her auburn hair hanging over her face. She was carrying a large basket full of wrapped candies.

"Hey, Dad," she announced, "I'm on the last bag." She stopped short when she saw her parents romancing in the arm chair. "Oh, no! Not again! Can't you two get a room?" She puckered up her face in disgust.

"Angela," said Rocky, standing now, almost at attention, "where did you ever hear such a banal expression?"

"Don't use those big English teacher words on me, Dad," responded his daughter, her oversized t-shirt hanging loosely around her knees, "every time I turn my back, you and Mom are acting like teenagers."

"And of course," smiled Pamela, gathering her papers and returning to her grading, "we wouldn't want to act like one of them." She looked directly at her 18-year-old daughter with a very pointed expression.

"Hey, Mom," queried Angela, "did the police find the murderer yet?" She pronounced "murderer" in a shaky, horror movie voice. Rocky scowled. He obviously didn't like either of his girls concerned with murderers. "Did you go back to the scene of the crime? What was it like?" asked Angela.

"I did and it looked like it always looks, Angie," she replied calmly, "Just a plain, ordinary lab filled with computers."

"Bor--ing," sang out Angela. "No blood?"

"No blood. Sorry, sweetie."

"Not a very interesting lab," Angie sighed. She plopped down on her parents' bed.

"And what would make a lab interesting, Angie?" queried Rocky, "Wires and beakers spewing dry ice? A mad scientist in a lab coat cackling gleefully?"

"That," answered Pamela, "would be some English teacher's dream of an interesting lab." She smiled.

"Dad," said Angela sitting up, obviously trying to be helpful to this adult lacking in real-world knowledge. "You have computer labs in the English Department too."

"Yes," continued Rocky, "but in the English Department we do not suck out our students' brains or give them lobotomies." He did his best Bela Lugosi imitation.

Angela grimaced at her father's lame attempt at horror humor.

"Nor do we," responded Pamela, "in the very humane Psychology Department."

"If by humane," he countered, "you mean that you reduce all emotions to multiple choice questions."

"Rocky," she sighed. "Not tonight. What is this, Halloween or something?"

"Sorry, Babe," said Rocky, hanging his head, and then added with a shrug, "just can't resist myself." He smiled at her, licking his lips, and she returned the smile.

"You two make me sick," snarled Angela, noticing the romantic spark between the couple. "Why do my parents always have to make google eyes at each other?" She was now sitting up on the bed, flipping the remaining pieces of candy in the bowl.

"I think that's goo-goo eyes," corrected Rocky.

"Wrong," challenged Pamela, laughing. "Everything is Google these days." They laughed together and Angela, unaware she was the subject of their joke, looked annoyed. Candide took advantage of the parents' distraction to jump up on the bed to beg for Angela's attention.

"Actually," said Angela, scratching Candide's head, and wary that she might not be taken seriously. "I'd like to see that lab some time. I mean, don't you think I should know about my mother's job?"

"Absolutely," responded Rocky, nodding. "I absolutely think you should know all about your mother's job. But that doesn't mean you have to hang out in that lab."

"I may just drop by some time to see what it looks like," She looked up at them to see their reaction. There was none.

"Or you could," said Pamela, "just take a Psychology class and then you could actually participate in one of our experiments in the lab."

"I could?" asked Angie, with delight, then suddenly hit with a new thought, "I wouldn't have to take your class, would I, Mom?"

"No," answered Pamela, laughing, "any psychology class would do."

"Come on," Rocky said, motioning to Angela, "scoot! Let your mother finish her grading. We're both disturbing her." He escorted the young woman out of the couple's bedroom.

Pamela smiled and was grateful for the brief recess from her otherwise dreary chore--and from the relentless stress of contemplating the contents of the secret in her pocketbook.

She thought about what her husband had said. Her colleagues in the department had been very considerate--very understanding. Many of them seemed to believe that she shouldn't have come in to work today.

After Mitchell's pronouncement about the entire department having sufficient animosity towards Charlotte to murder her, not much more had happened in her meeting with her Chair today. She wished she'd gotten an idea or at least a hint regarding the reason for the big fight between him and Charlotte yesterday, or the photograph that Charlotte had put in his mailbox. If these were issues that were causing Mitchell Marks any guilt, he didn't indicate as such to Pamela in his office this afternoon. No, Mitchell seemed as concerned about Charlotte's murder as the rest of them. But he didn't seem particularly guilt-ridden--at least, not to her. But, she wasn't a detective. How was she to know?

What she really wanted to do, needed to do, was examine the CD. But the computer was in their study which was right by the front door. If she suddenly stopped grading papers and went into the study to use the computer--for whatever reason—Rocky, and probably even Angie, would want to know what she was doing. It would just have to wait.

She frustratingly picked up the same paper she'd been grading for over an hour and tried again to pick out the student writer's main theme. Finally, after several more hours of bad grammar, poor vocabulary, and incredibly simplistic ideas, she finished the last paper with a flourish and placed it with the others in a manila folder. Then, she took the folder and her purse, with its forbidden treasure, and placed them both on the dining room table.

Returning to the bedroom, she quickly got ready for bed. She brushed her fine, chin-length hair, removing the tangles and making it shine. She brushed her teeth and rubbed her favorite smelling cream all over her face and arms. As she peeked out into the living room, she could see that Rocky was in the kitchen starting the dishwasher and turning off the lights.

"Is Angie...?"

"She went to bed a good hour ago," he whispered. "I guess all that Halloweening was exhausting." He came toward her in the bedroom, his arms extended for an embrace. After a goodnight kiss, she crawled into bed, yawning as she reached out to turn off her nightstand lamp. Rocky quickly got ready for bed and slipped in beside her. She remained very quiet and breathed regularly. Soon--amazingly soon, she always thought--Rocky was sound asleep, snoring gently. Candide, as if in sync with his master, timed his delicate doggie snores with Rocky's.

Pamela was rigid. She glanced at her nightstand clock with the digital face, discreetly trying not to move her body and disturb her husband. It was 11:20 p.m. She lay there listening to the snoring sounds beside and below her.

Again, she looked at the clock face. Now it read 11:45 p.m. Very carefully she pushed back the covers and gently slid her feet out, stepping into her slippers. Grabbing her robe from the back of the door, she quietly exited the bedroom, pulling the door shut behind her. She grabbed her purse from the dining table and walked softly down the hallway into the study.

Rocky had shut down the computer; she wished he hadn't done that, because the computer made the normal start-up noises when she pressed the power button. It couldn't be helped. She removed a pile of papers and clothing from the computer chair. She needed to clean up this room—some day. The kitchen was always immaculate because that was Rocky's domain and he kept it spotless. The rest of the house was hers and it showed. Her sloppy housekeeping bothered her, but not enough to actually work more industriously at it. She sat at the computer and reached into her purse for the CD. Removing the disk from its folder, she inserted the shiny circular disk into the CD drawer. Impatiently, she waited while the computer uploaded the data. She brought up her favorite acoustic analysis program and nervously loaded the data.

Immediately, the screen filled with a spectrograph and wavy lines, indicating the presence of sound. Some of the waves were rounded rather than sharp, indicating to Pamela's perceptive eye that she was looking at human vocal sound in addition to mechanical or non-human sound.

Placing a set of earplug speakers in her ears, she turned the volume control to a low level. She was totally engrossed in the screen in front of her as she moved her cursor to the start of the wavy line on the spectrograph and pressed *play*.

An unbelievably strange, guttural sound was emitted. It was hard to determine what it was or even describe it--like nothing she'd ever heard before. Certainly it was human, but it sounded like choking and there were also non-human sounds too--things being bumped, pushed, a double-clicking noise, a scraping, and various other sounds she couldn't identify. The entire visual display was comprised of these sounds.

Towards the end of the recorded section, the guttural, choking sound faded, as did the bumps and other noises. Finally, all the sounds ended abruptly. The wavy line on the spectrograph disappeared. Pamela clicked her cursor to indicate *stop*.

"What in God's name are you doing?" asked a voice.

She turned abruptly, petrified, her earplugs tumbling into her lap. Rocky was standing behind her. He'd entered quietly, while she was caught up in listening to the recording.

"Rocky!" she whispered, inhaling.

"What is that, Pamela?" he demanded. He used his drill sergeant voice—one she never liked.

"It's ... it's," she stammered, attempting to think of some way to explain what recording was so important that she'd kept it secret from her husband and had sneaked out of bed in the middle of the night to listen to.

"What is that?" he repeated, a look of horror, or maybe fury on his face.

"It's," she stammered, realizing that she wasn't going to be able to lie to her husband. "It's a recording of Charlotte's murder."

"What?" he shrieked in a whispered voice, not wanting to wake Angela.

"The master console in the lab automatically records anything when the toggle switch in a carrel is pushed. Charlotte must have bumped the toggle while she was being strangled and the system recorded it," she explained, quite reasonably, she thought.

"Okay," he said, hesitantly, "but what are you doing with it? Why did the police give it to you?"

"They didn't actually give it to me," she said, weakly, feeling more than a little guilty, "I recorded it. They don't know about it."

"What?" he yelped, again, trying to squelch his voice.

"I mean," she stuttered, "I mean, it just dawned on me this afternoon, that the system might have recorded the murder—if-- if Charlotte accidentally bumped the toggle switch on during the murder, an unlikely possibility. The police had already finished collecting evidence in the lab, Rocky. I wasn't doing anything wrong."

"Wrong!" he yelled, not being very successful in maintaining low tones, "You have a recording of the murder. You! The police don't know anything about it and you blithely bring it home to listen to. What do you intend to do with it? Solve the case yourself?"

"No, of course not," she protested. "I didn't even know what would be on it. It might have been all dead air, for all I knew. Rocky, this is what I do. This is my specialty. I understand about acoustic waves and how to analyze them. I think I can figure out what these sounds are. Maybe, if I can figure them out, it might help the police catch the killer."

"Are you crazy?" he huffed, "This is not some academic research project, Pammie. This is a murder. Somebody killed this woman and here you have a recording of them doing it. If they found out that you had this, your life would be in danger. As it is, your life is in jeopardy. I mean, you found the body. You can't go digging around the crime scene looking for clues. That could get you killed--just like Charlotte."

"Now, sweetheart," she said, touching his arms, "I appreciate your concern, really I do...."

He removed her hands, and placed his hands on her shoulders and looked pointedly in her eyes. "No. This is more than concern, Pamela. I want you to take this disk to the police first thing in the morning, tell them what it is, where and how you got it, and then leave it in their hands. Do you understand?"

"But ...."

"This isn't a request," he said, grimly. "I'm insisting. I'm insisting not only for your sake but for your daughter's sake--and mine too. What would Angie do without you? What would I do?"

"Nothing is going to happen to me," she said belligerently, "I'm fine and I can take care of myself."

"Pamela...."

Continuing to argue was useless, she realized. Besides, she was very tired.

"Oh, all right," she replied, relenting. "I'll take it to the police, if you insist."

"First thing in the morning."

"First thing," she agreed. Then, as they both seemed to be argued out, and as it was evident that he wasn't going to let her examine the disk, she removed it, replaced it in its sheath and returned it to her purse.

They went to bed again, quiet and tense. But Pamela didn't sleep well. She was grappling with how she would handle this. She wasn't about to give up on analyzing the disk now that she had it. And, on top of everything else, she had to get up extra early to attend a faculty meeting that promised to be anything but a touching tribute to the late Charlotte Clark.

Chapter 11

No, she wasn't late. Thank heavens. Her nerves were on edge and she'd hardly slept. Pamela entered the hallowed confines of the seminar room, where she'd held her acoustics class the night of the murder only a few days ago

It was already ten minutes after 7:00 a.m. on Thursday morning. So much for punctuality. Yet, she was the first to arrive. She scouted the room and staked out her favorite spot-- the side closest to the door. Just right, she thought, for a quick getaway, but with the best view of the campus's lovely elms. Setting down her purse on the floor beside her chair, she put her books, papers, and grade book on the table. Her light jacket, she placed over the back of the chair.

She pulled out the chair and was starting to sit when Arliss entered at breakneck speed, her ponytail bobbing up and down.

"Pam," she huffed, obviously out of breath, "My God, it's 7 o'clock in the morning! How can anyone function at such an hour? This will not be a pretty meeting." Arliss careened into the spot beside Pamela and let a stack of papers and books she'd been clutching slide precariously onto the table.

"Are they ever?" asked Pamela. "Do you know something I don't?"

"Now that Charlotte's not here to protest," said Arliss, dropping a folder and trying unsuccessfully to tuck a stray lock into her wayward hair, "I've decided to bring up the state of the animal lab to the entire faculty. I mean, everyone in this department has a vested interest in the welfare of our animals."

She slammed her remaining folders and papers on the spot next to Pamela and lurched into the chair, turning to Pamela, continuing her frenzy without missing a beat. "There's only so much one person can do. We have cages piled on top of each other. We simply don't have the funds to get the equipment to care for our animals properly, and yet there has been endless funding for that computer lab of Charlotte's! Now that she's not here to run roughshod over us, I don't see why some of that money can't be directed to our area."

Pamela nodded. "Has something new happened to get you so riled up?" she asked Arliss.

"We had six more rats die yesterday, and Dr. Goodman's youngest chimp is ill too. We aren't veterinarians and we simply don't have the funds to provide our animals with the proper conditions they need." She slouched in the chair, noticeably drained.

"Bring it up, by all means, but I suspect that Charlotte's demise will be the focus of this meeting."

At that moment, Joan entered the room.

"Ah!" she announced primly. "As usual, I see the women have arrived on time and the men are late."

"Joan," responded Pamela, "I might point out, that you're 15 minutes late."

"Yes, but the men never need to know that, do they, my dear?" Joan answered, her eyes twinkling.

"You're certainly cheerful for so early on such a grim occasion," Pamela smiled warmly.

"Dear girls," said Joan, taking a seat on the other side of Pamela, and carefully placing a large briefcase on the table before her. "It's a lovely fall day. Why not enjoy?" Then she neatly and almost formally sat in the chair, pulling herself as close to the table as possible. Pamela expected her to call the meeting to order.

"Ladies!" a booming voice called out as Willard entered, wearing a black suit with a black shirt and tie. He walked slowly and carefully, leaning on his wooden cane with the beautifully carved handle.

"Willard," greeted Joan, "Aren't you stylish."

"Dr. Swinton," said Arliss, "How are you?"

"Willard, did you wear that outfit trick-or-treating last night?" asked Pamela

"No, I'm just getting ready for Charlotte's memorial," responded Willard. "My, my. A roomful of lovely ladies all to myself. Now, that's what I get for arriving early," His round face and dimpled cheeks beamed as he bowed elegantly to each of the three women, "Dr. Barnes, Dr. Bentley, Miss MacGregor."

"You're 20 minutes late, Dr. Swinton," teased Arliss, noticeably warming under his friendly gaze.

"So I am, Miss MacGregor. However, I'm not used to arising at such an early hour. It's not a fit hour for man or beast, don't you agree?" He chuckled, puffing slightly, as he maneuvered his way into a chair at the near end of the table.

"Doesn't Miss MacGregor agree with what, Willard?" asked Bob Goodman, entering briskly. He pulled out the chair next to Arliss.

"Oh, that we academics are poor timekeepers, that's all, Dr. Goodman," responded Willard. He hung his cane carefully over the back of his chair.

"Willard, given that I'm uncharacteristically late, I'll have to agree with you--at least today," smiled Bob, as he opened a folder in front of him and handed a paper from it to Arliss. "Latest stats on Bailey" he whispered.

"I'm so sorry. So sorry," gasped Laura Delmondo, wearing a wispy, pastel-colored dress, entering immediately behind Goodman. "My alarm clock...traffic... sorry." She quickly floated to the opposite side of the table and slid with a dancer's grace into a chair.

"Good morning, Laura," greeted Pamela.

"Good morning," Laura responded. She fluffed her long blonde hair out over the back of her chair.

"Hmmph," scowled Arliss, slamming her own folders shut as she started reading the paper handed to her by Bob.

A loud, cheerful voice rang out from the hallway, singing *Proud Mary*, and Rex Tyson entered, sashaying his way around the table, all eyes turned to him--obviously just what he wanted, thought Pamela. He gave a mock blessing to all faculty members on either side of the table.

"Really, Rex," said Joan, "I believe you plan all your entrances for their most dramatic effect."

"Of course, dear lady!" chortled Tyson. He rounded the table, and as he reached Joan, he bent, grabbed her hand and gave it an air kiss.

Following on his heels, Phineas whined, "Rex, what about the second personality study?"

"Not now, Phineas," answered Rex, with a dismissing wave at the shorter man, "Just take a seat." Phineas frowned and took his seat, somewhat belligerently. Then, Rex pulled out a chair next to him and, rolling his leg over the top in the style of a bronco-rider straddling a horse, took his seat.

"Hello, Dr. Ottenback," said Pamela, greeting the small man.

"Yes, Phineas, how are things in the deviant personality area?" asked Bob Goodman.

Phineas nodded and gave a squinty smile.

"All right, faculty, we're late! We can never seem to get these meetings started on time!" announced Mitchell Marks as he entered rapidly, followed by Jane Marie, carrying a pile of papers. He walked determinedly to the chair at the head of the table and sat. Jane Marie plopped down the papers beside him and then quickly exited.

"All right," continued Marks, glancing around the table, "Who are we missing?"

"All present and accounted for, Boss!" reported Rex.

"Except, of course, Charlotte," added Willard. The group groaned softly.

"Now, people, you know the reason for this meeting. A horrible event has occurred. Dr. Clark was killed Tuesday night in our own computer lab. You've probably all been interviewed by now by the police. It's quite likely that you'll all have to answer additional questions as the police continue their investigation."

"Don't they know what happened yet?" asked Bob.

"What they appear to believe—and this is only supposition on my part because they aren't sharing their suspicions with me—is that Charlotte was working alone in the computer lab and someone unknown came in behind her and strangled her to death."

"Do they have any clues as to whom?" queried Joan.

"Not at the moment. They're considering everyone. The lab door was open, so apparently anyone—a worker, a student, a transient even—could have come in and killed her. But according to our own graduate student Kent Drummond who discovered the body, he locked the lab Tuesday afternoon when he left for the day. Now, we know that Charlotte liked to work late in the lab, but she typically always locked herself in. Of course, it's possible that she left the door open and the killer just walked in. But that seems unlikely."

"So, Mitchell, what do the police think is likely?" asked Pamela.

"They seem to think that Charlotte was locked in the lab and that the murderer unlocked the door quietly while Charlotte was working, entered, killed her, and then exited, leaving the door open after he or she left."

"But," said Laura, looking quizzical, "that would mean that the killer had a key to the lab." She looked around quizzically at all the people at the table who all looked as startled as she did.

"Right," confirmed Mitchell, nodding his head, "and you see where that puts us. Only faculty and a select few graduate students and Jane Marie have keys to the lab. I know I've been harping on lab security recently. My concern up until this point was the expensive equipment housed there; it never occurred to me that any of us were in danger when we were working there."

"I'm sure anyone could gain entrance to the lab—key or no key—if they were determined," added Rex.

"Yes," agreed Bob, "but, why? The police said nothing was stolen, so why would anyone need to get into the lab."

"That's exactly the point," added Mitchell, "The police seem to believe that the person wanted to kill Charlotte and succeeded."

The entire group was silent for several moments as they all looked at each other.

"All right, I'll say what all of you are thinking," spoke up Mitchell, breaking the silence. "Who would want to kill Charlotte? Few of us liked her. I've probably said it myself-- I could kill that woman. She drove me crazy, I'll admit it. She probably drove a lot of you crazy. But someone actually did kill her."

"And it looks like it was one of us," said Willard, looking around at his colleagues.

"Well, it wasn't me," snarled Arliss, "although I congratulate whoever did do it."

"Arliss!" gasped Pamela.

"Admit it, Pam," responded Arliss, "No one liked her."

"But you don't kill people just because they're unpleasant," added Joan.

"Stop! Stop!" yelled Mitchell, as the group erupted into argument. "Who killed Charlotte is not for us to determine. We have more pressing concerns."

"What could be more pressing than finding Charlotte's killer?" asked Willard.

"Yes," agreed Laura, "None of us are safe until the killer is found."

"I disagree," stated Mitchell, to the consternation of the group. "I don't know who killed Charlotte, but it was obviously for an unknown and very specific reason. As far as I know, I haven't antagonized any of you to the point that any of you wish me dead—at least I don't think I have. Therefore, I'm really not afraid. That doesn't mean I won't be cautious. And I suggest you all be especially cautious too. For one thing, I suggest none of us use the lab late at night—particularly alone. Actually, I suggest none of us work alone in the building after hours at all. If we take these simple precautions and use common sense we should all be fine. At least, until the police make an arrest. Can we all agree to take these precautions?"

The group looked around at each other and all mumbled their agreement.

"What about Charlotte?" asked Joan. "Has anyone thought at all about her or is the purpose of this meeting merely to protect ourselves?"

"Actually," continued Marks, "That's the second reason I called this meeting. I have contacted Charlotte's next of kin…"

"She had relatives?" asked Bob.

"They probably all disowned her," added Arliss.

"She had a younger sister," continued Mitchell, ignoring Arliss. "They were evidently estranged—although she was Charlotte's sole heir and receives the bulk of her estate after several magnanimous gifts to Grace University. Anyway, the sister has been contacted by the administration and she is taking care of funeral arrangements which will be private at the sister's home in Ohio. Therefore, we will not need to attend. However, that does not mean that we should do nothing. Charlotte was the major financial bastion of this department and probably of this university. We must honor her in some way. I have decided that we will hold a memorial service for her in the campus chapel. We will invite the sister, although I doubt she'll come. We, of course, will all attend." Mitchell said this last comment with a stern voice and a piercing look at each individual faculty member.

"When are you planning to hold this memorial, Mitchell?" questioned Pamela.

"As soon as possible," he replied. "Jane Marie is trying to reserve the chapel for the next day or so. We will keep you all informed and I expect you to clear your schedules so you can attend, and encourage your students to attend too. We owe this much to Charlotte. We may not have liked her—but we all certainly liked what she did for us and for this university."

The group sat in silence. They couldn't argue with the truth.

"Are there any other concerns that relate to Charlotte?" He looked around.

Arliss rose and said, "I'd like to discuss funding for the animal lab."

"Concerns that relate to Charlotte," repeated Mitchell, staring directly at Arliss who sat back down quickly, glaring at Mitchell and breathing audibly.

"If not, this meeting is adjourned." He bowed his head briefly, almost as if he were offering a benediction, and then exited quickly.

Chapter 12

"Dr.Barnes!   Dr. Barnes!" the student repeated.   Pamela snapped out of her reverie and was drawn back into her classroom. She was leaning against her desk at the front of the small classroom on the second floor. It was Thursday morning, not long after the sunrise faculty meeting, and she was trying to lecture to her undergraduate research class, but not having much success.

"Now," she said, "where was I?"   She grabbed her coffee cup and took a quick sip. This was a teacher's trick she used to give herself a moment to gather her thoughts--thoughts that were roaming far from the class discussion today.

"Dr. Barnes," said the girl, with increased emphasis, "you were talking about human subjects." The young woman smiled self-righteously as she looked around the room.

"Yes," said Pamela, "now, being as how we psychologists conduct our research primarily on human beings.... I know, I know, Dr. Goodman would include all those animals too. But, for the most part, psychologists deal with humans and when we gather data we collect it from humans. That presents us with certain problems that other scientists don't have to deal with, right?" She looked around the room expectantly. Several hands rose.

"You have to be really careful with people," said one young man.

"That's true, Michael," responded Pamela, "how so?"

"You can't do anything to humans without their consent," added a girl, seated close to Michael.

"You mean," posed Pamela, "that if I got someone's consent I could do anything I wanted?"

"No," continued Michael, the ball now in his corner, "psychologists can't just go out and start conducting experiments on people because they want to."

"They can't?" exclaimed Pamela.

"No," added the girl, "psychologists have to get permission before they do an experiment." She nodded, satisfied with her answer.

"Permission from whom?" questioned Pamela, smiling, "The government? The head of their department? Their parents?"

The class giggled and looked around. No hands were raised. Most students now focused on their desktops.   Pamela recognized the "I don't have a clue what the answer is" stare.

"Where do you think they should get permission," she suggested.

"The police," said one of her smart-alecks by the window. The entire class laughed. Pamela, however, was immediately drawn back to her personal thoughts. The last thing she'd told her husband before they went to bed last night was that she'd take the CD of Charlotte's murder to the police first thing this morning before the 7 a.m. meeting, but she hadn't done so. It was still in her purse in her office. True, she'd planned to do it—she'd even driven towards Police Headquarters on her way to work, but then, she'd suddenly changed her mind--she didn't know why--and backtracked to campus.

Now, here she was in her Thursday morning class feeling guilty that she hadn't kept her word to Rocky and wondering what she should do about it. She knew she must take the disk to the police, but she was procrastinating and she didn't know why.

"Dr. Barnes," whined the same girl who'd interrupted Pamela's daydreaming earlier. "Dr. Barnes, what should we do?"

"What?" asked Pamela, suddenly confused. It was almost as if the student was privy to her thoughts and was asking her what she was going to do about the CD.

"Dr. Barnes," said the girl, "you don't seem like yourself today."

"No, Dr. Barnes," agreed another student near the front. "Maybe you're having a delayed reaction to Dr. Clark's death."

Delayed reaction, oh my, Pamela thought. Students never failed to toss in some tidbit of knowledge they'd picked up in one of their other classes.

"Dr. Barnes," said another, "maybe you should go home and get some rest. You look a little drained."

For heaven's sake, Pamela smiled to herself; she'd better pull it together. "I'm just fine," she said. "Now, what I think you're looking for is The Human Subjects' Committee. Every large research university has one and it's devoted to reviewing any proposed research that involves humans. We have one here at Grace University. The Human Subjects' Committee is somewhat like an enforced conscience for researchers. It ensures that all research is ethical. What do you think about that?"

"I think it's really important," said one young woman, "because you sometimes hear about scientists who are more concerned with their studies than with the people involved."

"Right," agreed another girl, "just because a person is a scientist doesn't mean that they're automatically ethical."

Pamela nodded. Just because a person is a scientist doesn't mean they're automatically ethical, she thought, nor does it mean they automatically know what the ethical thing to do is in any particular situation. She bit her lip. She should just hop in her car and take the CD to Shoop right now and be over with it.

"All right," she said to the group, "Let's see if you've read this chapter on research ethics. Get in your discussion groups and work on the problems on page 246 in your textbook. You can have the rest of the class period to do it and when you've answered all the questions, bring your written responses to me before you leave." The students began moving their desks around into small groups of four or five and were soon talking quietly among themselves.

Pamela returned to the chair behind her desk and continued sipping her coffee. She peered out the classroom window onto the campus grounds. It was a beautiful fall day--the first day of November. From here, she could see Meer Hall, the biology building and Drucker Hall, the math building. Beyond Drucker, was Silverton Hall, the English building, where her husband worked. She could hear students walking on the sidewalks below, chatting and enjoying the crisp air. The gruesome events of two days ago appeared far from their thoughts.

She thought of the CD she played last night on her home computer screen and how the wave form of the recorded sound appeared in the sound analysis program. It was the familiar soft curve of human vocal sound, but there were non-human noises there too. What were they? She really needed to listen to it again. Maybe she could figure out what the sounds were and somehow figure out who the killer was. Maybe Charlotte's choking sounds contained some information--she didn't know what--but something that might provide some information. She wanted to know, to help. But she'd promised Rocky that she'd take the CD to the police today--first thing. And she hadn't. She'd lied--well, not exactly lied. She intended to take it to the police, but she couldn't--she just couldn't.

When the students started to collect their books and put them in their backpacks--always a sign that class was nearing its official end, she checked her watch. The groups started coming up and showing her their work. Virtually all groups had answered the questions correctly. She smiled. She may have been off in dreamland, but the lesson of the day had penetrated.

Saying her farewells to her students, she grabbed her belongings, and headed down the hallway to her office. As she rounded the corner, she spotted Willard in Joan's office chatting amiably. A wave at her two friends and she continued on. After she entered her office and had made herself comfortable at her desk, her phone rang.

"Dr. Barnes," sang Jane Marie, "Are you up to no good?" Pamela was briefly startled because, unbeknownst to Jane Marie, no good was obviously what Pamela was up to.

"No," she replied, "I'm just sitting here. Thought I'd eat lunch."

"If you'd like some juicy news," said Jane Marie, in her lowest gossipy voice, "I think I may have found out who the woman in the photograph is--you know, the one that Dr. Clark put in Dr. Marks's mailbox before she was murdered."

"Who?" asked Pamela.

"I did some snooping," she whispered. "I found her photograph in a yearbook from about ten years back."

"You mean she's a student?" cried Pamela.

"It appears so—or was," said Jane Marie, "Her name is Evelyn Carrier. Does that ring a bell?"

"No," replied Pamela, "I've never heard of her. Why would Charlotte put some former student's photo in Mitchell's mailbox with no note or anything? It's weird."

"Particularly when she's murdered the next day," said Jane Marie.

"Jane Marie," said Pamela, "a question. Did you happen to mention to Detective Shoop about this photograph?"

"No," said Jane Marie, "I figured I'd leave that for Dr. Marks to do. He has the photo--or rather it's on his desk. I don't know if he did or didn't tell Shoop. Do you?"

"No," said Pamela. "Shoop is closed mouthed just like Mitchell. He asks questions, but he surely doesn't offer much information."

"That's for sure," responded Jane Marie.

"Listen," suggested Pamela, "I'm not saying we intentionally try to get Mitchell in hot water, but if Shoop doesn't know about the photo--or about the fight between Mitchell and Charlotte-- don't you think someone should tell him?"

"You mean me?" asked Jane Marie, horrified. "I value my job."

"Hmmm," said Pamela, thoughtfully, "Oh, don't worry; I understand if you don't want to get involved, but I think Shoop ought to know. Listen, Jane Marie, please don't say anything about this discussion to Mitchell."

"Don't worry," the secretary replied, "I won't. Bye." Pamela hung up as she heard Jane Marie's receiver click off.

Why hadn't she told Shoop about the fight or the photograph? Maybe she'd gotten so worked up about listening to the CD that she wasn't even thinking about any other potentially important information related to the murder. This, she resolved, was not behaving responsibly--or ethically. She decided she'd do what she'd promised her husband she would--not only that—she'd fill Shoop in on these other tidbits that may or may not be related to Charlotte Clark's murder. It was the least she could do. She was an ethical person, after all.

Chapter 13

She moved over to her couch where she could relax. The couch was very soft and comfortable--as Detective Shoop had discovered. The afternoon was waning, and as she looked out her window, she could see the beautiful reds and yellows of autumn in the south. She was still in her office, waiting for her office hours to end so she could take the controversial disk to the police.

As she poured herself another cup of Rocky's home brewed tea from her thermos, Kent appeared at her door. Oh, God! She'd forgotten the young man again. How unconscionable of her, when it was Kent who'd discovered Charlotte's body. Good grief, she thought, he'd undergone as much interrogation as she had and was probably suffering as much emotional trauma. She should have checked up on him to see how he was coping. It was reneging on her responsibilities as his advisor and supervisor and here he was at her door, probably upset.

"Kent," she said, rising and inviting him in. "Please, have a seat." She indicated the chair, but the young man remained standing.

"That's okay, Dr. Barnes," he said, anxiously. "I just wanted to touch base with you." He looked down in hesitation. "I just stopped by to let you know that I contacted our research subjects for this week and rescheduled them all for next week." He wrapped the cord from a set of headphones that hung around his shoulders like a totem around his fingers. "You know, I thought they might be upset about Dr. Clark's death and...also, I wasn't absolutely sure when the police would be out of the lab."

"That's a good idea, Kent," said Pamela, "Thank you. The police should be finished in the lab soon, if they aren't already."

"I was just down there, Dr. B," he reported enthusiastically, "and they're gone. The tape is down."

"Great. So, when do we start collecting again?"

"Monday," he replied, "We'll have to double up, but it's not a problem 'cause we have plenty of space in the lab and there aren't any other studies scheduled in there for the next two weeks. I checked."

"Great," she said, smiling. "I'm relieved that you took it upon yourself and did that."

Suddenly, Angela meandered into the doorway.

"Hey," greeted Kent, "I bet you're looking for the sign-up sheet for Dr. Barnes' experiment."

"Uh, no," responded Angela, shyly, "I was looking for my...for Dr. Barnes."

"She's here; you're in luck," he quipped.

At that, Angela spotted her mother seated on her blue and pink sofa and her mother spotted her.

"Sweetie! What are you doing here?" she asked. "Kent, this is my daughter, Angela. She's a freshman here at Grace University. Angie, this is Kent Drummond, my top graduate assistant."

"Gee, Dr. B, I'm honored," he beamed, "Hello, Angie. Dr. B talks about you all the time, so I feel like I know you already."

"Mom," cringed Angela, "I wish you wouldn't talk about me to your students."

"Hey, Angie, "continued Kent, "Don't worry. She only says nice things. You sound like a great girl from what I can tell."

Angela beamed and blushed. Pamela felt like an unwelcome intruder at this moment.

"Listen, honey," Pamela began, "Did you want a ride home? I can't leave right this minute. Do you want to stick around and wait for me?"

"I ...uh..." stammered Angela.

"I know, Dr. B," said Kent, cutting in, obviously in a hurry to get going. "I'm free now that we've cancelled our subjects for the day. I was heading out. I'll be happy to give you a ride home, Angie. If you don't mind riding in my old clunker." He grinned sheepishly, the purple highlights in his prickly-looking hair gleaming.

"I guess. Is it okay, Mom?" asked Angela

"It's fine with me, Kent, if you're sure you're not too busy."

"Not a problem! Let's go, Angie!" With that, and swinging the headphones back over his shoulder, he turned abruptly and skated off on his sneaker-clad feet, Angela following in his tracks.

Pamela watched her daughter go off with the young man. Seeing the headphones draped around his shoulders, Pamela suddenly pictured Charlotte, dead in the lab with a set of similar headphones wrapped around her neck. She thought, could Kent possibly be the killer? Oh, she was being ridiculous! She realized that she often saw Kent in the building carrying headphone units—just like the set that had strangled Charlotte. But, he worked in the lab. He fixed defective equipment; he was probably repairing that set of headphones that he was wearing around his neck. But, Charlotte was strangled with a headphone set and certainly Kent had access to those; he was also in the building the night of the murder. Was it possible? Could Kent have killed Charlotte? And here she'd sent her daughter off with him. Oh, for heaven's sake. This was truly ridiculous! Kent was in her class all Tuesday night. If he had murdered Charlotte, he would have had to leave her class, run to the lab, murder Charlotte, and then run back to get her—all in the space of just a few minutes. He simply wasn't gone long enough to do all of that. And, besides, why? Why would he kill Charlotte? He had no motive. She was letting her mind run crazy.

Pamela breathed deeply. Back to reality, she told herself. Kent was a wonderful assistant; she was lucky. As she considered her recent conversation with the young man, she realized suddenly that the lab was now totally empty. No other faculty members were collecting data there as Kent had informed her, the police were done with their work, and subjects for Pamela's study wouldn't be in there until next week. The lab was locked for now--with all its secrets of Charlotte's demise. Probably all for the best, she thought. Allow some time to pass and maybe people won't be uncomfortable about having to go in there. Of course, Mitchell had warned the faculty about working alone in the lab—but he said at night, and it was the middle of the afternoon.

Glancing at her watch, she realized that it was past her office hours. She was free to leave. She gathered her belongings together and headed out. Willard's door was closed but Joan, she noticed, was sitting at her desk, typing, and sipping a cup of tea, the stringed label from her tea bag hanging over the edge of her porcelain cup. Pamela stopped at her door.

"Oh, my," said Joan, looking up, smiling, the light reflecting on her rimless reading glasses, "I was so engrossed, I didn't see you standing there." Pamela came into her office and perched on the edge of Joan's upholstered arm chair. She and Joan must look as if they were vying for "most comfy office" honors. Joan's husband had died over five years ago and Joan's two sons had been on their own for years—in distant states, much to Joan's everlasting dismay. There were photographs of several grandchildren festooning Joan's desk.

"So," Pamela said to her friend, "back at work?"

"Not that I ever stopped," chuckled Joan, her buoyant good humor rippling out. She sipped her tea.

"We're allowed some time to mourn for Charlotte," noted Pamela, not totally facetiously, giving Joan a biting glance.

"Have a cookie," Joan said, offering Pamela a delicate frosted biscuit from a tray of goodies.

"Joan," chided Pamela, "you know I'm trying to diet." She tapped her tummy.

"You're always trying to diet," responded Joan, "and it's totally unnecessary. Come now, one little cookie. See how small they are."

"I really shouldn't," Pamela hesitated, "I need to get home."

"Now, if you're worried about your diet," said Joan broadly, "that's just the place not to go. You know that military man of yours will feed you some of his Army chow the minute you walk in the door." Joan knew that Rocky never prepared "chow." In fact, she knew that Rocky would be horrified at her use of that term. He was a gourmet cook—and no one better forget it. Pamela selected a little pink wafer.

"Right," answered Pamela, "I swear he's determined to make me a blimp."

"Are we still on for our girls' night out on Friday?" Joan asked, looking down to double check something she'd written on her computer. All Pamela could see was the top of her well-coiffed white hair.

"As far as I know," said Pamela, "I'll double check with Arliss. Yum." She popped the remaining piece of cookie into her mouth.

"I hope," said Joan, "that you were joking about taking time out to mourn for Charlotte. I believe the only mourning we should do is a good toast to her soul at *Who-Who's*. And, of course, a eulogy or two at her memorial on Sunday."

"Joan," said Pamela, scowling. "You sound as if you're happy she's dead."

"Heavens' no," laughed Joan, "Charlotte may have driven most of the department crazy, but she didn't bother me at all. I understood her."

"You did?" asked Pamela, "How so?" She reached for another cookie.

"Well," whispered Joan, inclining her head towards Pamela, "It may have appeared at times that Charlotte was running roughshod over Mitchell--and she certainly was trying to--but that doesn't necessarily mean that she was successful. Although, I'll admit I did cheer some of her efforts in skewering our chief-- or any of our male faculty members--if truth be told." Joan looked back at her monitor, leaving Pamela to decipher her cryptic words.

"What are you talking about Joan?"

"Pamela," continued Joan, "there were--are--things going on in this department of which you're probably not aware."

"Such as?"

"Dear, dear," whispered Joan, "I'm really not at liberty to discuss them, but suffice it to say, there is small battle of the sexes in progress."

"What do you mean 'battle of the sexes'?"

"My understanding is that it centers on this tenure thing," said Joan. "Rumor has it that the Dean has restricted our department to two--not three candidates."

"Yes," nodded Pamela. "I've heard as much. So, what is it? Mitchell and Charlotte were feuding about which two?"

"Among other things," said Joan, mysteriously. "He wants me to take over as Tenure Committee Chair." She rolled her eyes.

"Congratulations! Lucky you," said Pamela.

"Thank you," replied Joan, biting her lip, "I just hope I don't end up the same as Charlotte did." Pamela frowned at her.

"The Tenure Committee--do you think that's why she was murdered?" questioned Pamela.

"She certainly was consumed by it. At least making sure Laura got tenure. If the Dean truly was forcing her to restrict our department to two candidates, that would put Charlotte in a very awkward position," reasoned Joan.

"I always assumed that Charlotte thought highly of Laura. Surely she would fight for her to get tenure."

"Maybe," said Joan, "but, did you hear Charlotte and Laura going at it earlier this week?"

"No," said Pamela, moving closer to her friend.

"It was awful!" explained Joan. "I've heard Charlotte rage like that before, but usually to a student. Laura is so sweet."

"Why would she do that?" questioned Pamela.

"Charlotte has invested so much time and effort into making Laura--as Charlotte saw it--what Laura is today. Now, Laura is spending all her time, or what Charlotte evidently saw as 'all her time,'" and here Joan looked around before she leaned close to Pamela and whispered, "trying to get pregnant rather than trying to get published."

"And trying to get published is ever so much more important?" concluded Pamela, facetiously.

"In Charlotte's eyes," stated Joan. "Why wouldn't it be? That's all Charlotte lived for? Her career. She had no husband, no family. Laura was like a daughter to her."

"It doesn't sound like she treated her like a daughter," said Pamela.

"I agree," nodded Joan. "If Laura were my daughter I'd be giving her all the moral support she needed for this baby enterprise. My goodness, she shouldn't need much encouragement. With that sexy hunk Vittorio for a husband, I'd think getting pregnant would be relatively easy."

"But, I've been hearing that Laura was using *in vitro* to get pregnant," noted Pamela. In fact, she'd heard it from Laura herself.

"Yes, I've heard that," answered Joan. "Poor dear. Rumor has it that she and Vittorio have been trying this *in vitro* thing for several rounds now. So far, no success. Laura is a darling, and she does top-notch research. She didn't deserve a dressing down from Charlotte."

"I know," responded Pamela. "I just don't get it."

"It must have been because of the upcoming tenure meeting," added Joan. "Something tells me that Charlotte, as Chair, knew something that we committee members don't. Probably this business with the cut-back in the number of candidates the Dean is willing to accept. Charlotte may just have been trying to prepare Laura for a letdown. I mean, with all the baby making efforts, Laura's publication output has slipped this year. At least, it's definitely less than Rex's and Phin's. That may be why Charlotte was demanding that all three candidates include their dissertations in their portfolios."

"That's ridiculous!" snorted Pamela. "No one on the Committee has time to read one, let alone three, dissertations."

"No, of course not," agreed Joan, "It was all just for show. And to provide Charlotte a way to demonstrate her clout."

"You won't make the committee read the dissertations, will you?"

"Never!" replied Joan.

"You don't think that Charlotte pushed Laura so far that Laura just pushed back?" asked Pamela, peeking out of the corner of her eye for Joan's reaction.

"I don't think Laura could hurt a fly," responded Joan. "Charlotte annoyed so many people, Pamela. I wouldn't put it past her to have antagonized someone--anyone--not even necessarily someone on campus--so badly that that person followed her into the lab and 'offed' her."

"Joan!" cried Pamela, "offed?"

"I'm just trying out the appropriate lingo," responded Joan, brushing a few cookie crumbs from the front of her lace blouse.

"So you don't think the killer could be someone in the department like Mitchell said?" asked Pamela carefully.

"Of course not," responded Joan, "I can't imagine anyone in our department doing such a thing. It's probably an irate student who got an 'F' or a clerk in a store Charlotte browbeat--or even," she bent her head low and whispered, "even a scorned lover."

"Joan," laughed Pamela, "you read too many mysteries. Charlotte was married to her job. Besides, she'd emasculate any man who attempted to have sex with her."

"My dear you are delicious," smirked Joan.

"Not as delicious as your cookies," said Pamela lifting her eyebrows and joining in the hearty laughter. The chuckling of the two women could be heard up and down the hallway.

The tell-tale computer voice on Joan's PC announced "You've got mail!" and Joan clicked on the envelope icon.

"Wonderful!" she scowled, reading the new email message.

"What?" asked Pamela.

"The Charlotte Clark memorial service is scheduled for this Sunday afternoon at 2:00 p.m..at the campus chapel." She drummed her fingers on her keyboard. "I'm almost tempted to send my regrets." She placed her fingers in a keyboard-ready position.

"Now, Joan," warned Pamela, reaching out her hand and placing it on Joan's keyboard fingers, "You know Mitchell expects us all there. It won't be so bad. We can sit together." Joan removed her hands from her computer, resignedly.

"At least we have *Who-Who's* to look forward to!" she added, cheerfully.

When Pamela finally left Joan's office it was getting late. Pamela realized that Rocky would be wondering where she was. She headed down the side staircase and onto the main floor, noticing immediately that the side hallway leading to the lab appeared deserted. Rex's, Phin's, and the grad students' offices were all closed. The building seemed empty.

Pamela quickly slipped down the hallway toward the lab. Just as Kent had said, the police tape had been removed. Unlocking the door, she moved inside, and closed the door behind her. As she looked around, she realized she was alone--as she expected she would be--given what Kent had told her about rescheduling her subjects for next week. She went to the master console and reached into the side drawer from which she withdrew a blank CD.

She moved carefully to the first row of computers--scrupulously avoiding #4--where Charlotte Clark had died. She stopped at #10, the furthest away from #4, in the first row. She pulled out the chair and sat down. Here she could see much of what Charlotte probably saw two nights ago. Not much. The acoustic battening walls of the carrel surrounded her. She reached inside her purse for the infamous computer disk. After powering up the computer, she opened a CD drawer, inserted her disk, and placed the blank disk in a second drawer. On the start up screen, she clicked on "copy disk" and pressed "enter." It was possible to burn disks on her office computer, but she knew the administration was able to (and probably did) keep a record of all faculty activity on their office computers. It was much safer to make duplicate copies (particularly this one) in the lab. The computer whirred and spun and the lights on the two drawers flickered. She was entranced watching the duplication process when she heard the door to the lab open.

Chapter 14

The noise was soft but unmistakable. Someone had unlocked and opened the door to the lab. Had she locked the door behind her when she entered? She was sure she had. The mysterious person obviously had a key. Without thinking, she stood up at the carrel where she was working.

"Hello," she called out cheerily. "I'm working in here! It's Dr. Barnes!" She waited for someone to enter but the door was quickly closed.

Pamela looked down briefly at the progress on the CD duplication. When the light clicked off, she opened both drawers and removed the original CD and the duplicate, and slipped them in their sleeves and into her purse. Waiting to see if the person on the other side of the door would change his or her mind and enter the lab, she remained standing in the carrel, breathless. After a few minutes, which seemed like a few hours, she headed for the door.

Cautiously turning the knob, she peeked out, and seeing no one in the hallway, she slipped out, and turned back to lock the door behind her. As she turned around, she found herself staring into the face of Willard Swinton who'd just come up behind her.

"Pamela," he began.

"Willard," she spoke, breathlessly, shocked to see him appear seemingly out of nowhere. "I didn't see you. Did you just open the lab door?"

"The door? No. I was in the men's restroom," he explained. His dimples indenting his dark cheeks like a chocolate mousse. "Sorry to have scared you. You weren't working in the lab, were you? If it were me I'd stay far, far away from that place."

"I..." she stammered, "I have data to collect...." She started to walk past him.

"Pamela," he called out, touching her arm, "Could I have just a word with you?"

"I ...." she sputtered, anxious to get going and very conscious of the contraband in her purse. "I guess, all right. I'm in a bit of a hurry, though."

"Of course," he said sweetly. "I simply wanted to get your views on our tenure problems now that Charlotte is...."

"Yes," said Pamela, "yes, of course. I really hadn't thought about that, Willard. I guess I'll have to. We do have three candidates waiting on our decision."

"We do," he noted, "and now that Charlotte is...um...out of the picture...well, I'm afraid our decision is going to be even more difficult."

"How?" she asked.

"You may have heard," he began, "that the Dean is talking of restricting our department to two tenure appointments instead of three."

"I had heard that," she said.

"And with Charlotte gone, there are now only four members on the Tenure Committee. If there's a split vote--and there may be--how will we come to a decision?"

"Willard," she answered, sighing, "Let's get past this horrible event. Charlotte is barely dead. I just can't think right now about how her death will affect my committee vote."

"Pamela," he said softly, his cheeks flattening, the dimples gone, "You're so right. This has been such a terrible ordeal for you ...finding her body. I never should have even mentioned this to you. I'm so sorry." He bent his head and looked genuinely grieved.

"It's all right, Willard," she said, "truly it is. But, can't we talk about it later? I really need to get going. It's getting late and ...."

"Yes, I'm so sorry," he replied. "I'll talk to you next week. We have plenty of time to discuss this. Maybe you and Joan and I can get together and...."

"Yes," she nodded, now walking away and calling back to him, "we'll do that. Bye!" She strode down the hallway and out the corner entrance and into the parking lot. Even inside her car she was unable to calm down. Not that Willard Swinton bothered her. He was a dear, sweet, gentle soul. It was just that she was so nervous about making the duplicate CD. It was as if all eyes were on her, and then to bump into him right as she left the lab. It was as if he appeared out of nowhere. It was simply unnerving. Had he been the one who opened the lab door? And if so, why did he deny it when she asked him?

She started her engine and bolted out of the lot. No one seemed to be looking at her as she left. Thank goodness. Oh, she was becoming paranoid. Now, she thought, off to the police station.

The local police headquarters-court house was located in the downtown area, several blocks from campus and around the corner from the Reardon Coffee Factory. Pamela had actually been there many times, to pay derelict traffic fines—of which she had accumulated many. Rocky called her Lead Foot because of her penchant for driving over the speed limit. Maybe that's why she was procrastinating in bringing the CD to Shoop. The place reminded her of one of her embarrassing flaws—she was a bad driver. She tended to drift off and think of anything other than the road or—worse—she'd allow her emotions to bleed into her pedal foot—particularly angry emotions—and before she realized it, she was speeding. It happened far more often than she cared to realize. The tickets in the mail were enough of a reminder, but having to come here to the local courthouse/police station—was just too much.

There it was. An old concrete building stuck on the corner. It looked like some dilapidated public school built in the 50's--ochre in color, two stories, with grey porticos. Imposing but not very elegant. A small parking lot was in front. One section of the lot was labeled "Visitors." She found an empty spot in this section, parked, and with a gulp headed toward the police entrance on the parking lot side.

Inside the building, the place was busy. Uniformed officers were moving around. Some workers were seated at desks out in the open, and some she could see in offices to either side of the large central area. She walked up to a counter that was manned by a uniformed officer.

"May I help you, ma'am?" he asked.

"I'd like to see Detective Shoop, if he's in," she responded.

"One moment," the officer answered, leaving her there, and heading off towards the back of the central area to one of the side offices. He disappeared into a doorway and soon came out followed by Shoop. Pamela would recognize that tall, loping gait anywhere. The two men walked to the counter.

"Dr. Barnes," greeted Shoop, wiping his nose with his large handkerchief and then stuffing it in his jacket pocket. "Seems you know your way around here, so I hear."

"What?" she gulped.

"One of my friends in Traffic tells me they have a Pamela Barnes who has racked up quite a record of fines. Would that be you?"

"I don't see what my driving record has to do with a murder case."

He gave her a Cheshire Cat smile and held out his hand which she shook very unwillingly. "It doesn't. Have you remembered anything else?"

"Yes," she said, "and I have something for you."

"Oh?" he said, sounding intrigued, "Well, then, why don't you come back to my office."

He led the way and Pamela followed him, trying vainly to keep up with his long strides. When they reached his office, Shoop stood aside and held the door for her to enter. It was a glum looking room, smelling of mentholated spray and spearmint. There was a small humidifier in the corner spewing steam. Shoop removed some papers and magazines from a green plastic couch and gestured for her to sit. She did so cautiously as the furniture looked as if it had been donated from a rummage sale. Shoop returned to his desk and pulled a lozenge from a jar and popped it in his mouth.

"Sorry," he said, "Got a bit of a cold. Now, Dr. Barnes, you say you have something for me?"

"Detective," she began, "First, let me say, that after your men were finished going over our computer lab, I went down there to look around. I got to thinking."

"Not always a wise thing, eh?" he chuckled.

"Probably not," she responded, "as I'm not sure you'll approve of what I've done. I know my husband doesn't."

"Hmm," he said, "this is sounding more and more interesting."

"Anyway," she continued, "I was in the lab today." She surely wasn't going to tell him that she'd broken in yesterday before the crime scene tape was removed. "and I thought about what might have happened when Charlotte was ...was ...when she died. I thought it was probably likely that there would've been a struggle. You see, each computer desk in the first row has a toggle switch for recording."

"Yes," he added, "I realize that. But the toggle switch in the carrel where Dr. Clark was found was off."

"I know," Pamela continued, "but I speculated that if during the struggle between Charlotte and her killer--surely there must have been a struggle--what if the killer pushed Charlotte down on the desk or if she pushed her hands down to get leverage--or any number of possibilities--and accidentally pushed the toggle switch."

"Even so, Dr. Barnes," Shoop replied, "the toggle switch just turns the sound on and off--it doesn't actually start a recording. Our crime techs have gone all over that computer."

"I know," she said, feeling somewhat exasperated, "I use that lab all the time. But what you don't know, Detective, is that the master console makes back-up recordings anytime a toggle switch is turned on. These back-up recordings are erased at regular intervals when it's determined that they're no longer needed. Usually a graduate assistant does that."

"I see," he nodded.

"So," she said, "I thought, just on the off chance that maybe there was a back-up recording made of the murder--or even a part of the murder--that it might be worth it to just check those back-up recordings for the period when the murder probably took place."

"And?" he queried, his big brows lifting skyward, the lozenge rolling in his mouth.

"A back-up did record briefly on Tuesday night at 8:27 p.m., in Carrel #4--about two minutes worth of sound." She reached into her purse and brought out the original CD in its paper sleeve.

He reached out for the CD, saying smugly, "You are the little scientist, aren't you?"

"That's my job, yes," she replied.   She sat quietly then, as Shoop examined the disk.   He bit his lip, obviously thinking about what to do next. Then, shrugging, he slid the disk out of the sleeve, pressed the CD drawer on his small, desktop computer and loaded the disk.

"I take it, you've listened to it," he looked at her.

"Yes," she said, "I didn't want to bother bringing it here if it didn't have anything on it."

"Okay," he said. "Let's see what all the fuss is about." He brought up his *Sound Player* and hit "enter." From the built-in speaker on his computer, the choking sounds of Charlotte Clark, plus the extraneous bumps, scratches, and clicks that Pamela had also heard when she first played the brief recording sprang to life.   Soon the sounds ceased as abruptly as they started.

"That's it?" he asked, pulling his large cloth handkerchief out of his pocket and again rubbing his nose.

She cringed. If she stayed in this office much longer, she'd surely catch some wayward bacteria. "That's it."

"It does seem to be the sound of someone choking," he noted. "I'll have forensics take a look at it. If they think it warrants further investigation, they'll probably go back and extract the data from your master console themselves." He removed the CD from the drawer and slid it back into the sleeve.

"Detective," Pamela spoke rapidly, fearing that Shoop would not heed her ideas, "I think you can clearly hear Charlotte struggling on this recording. It's possible that she might be trying to say something--maybe sending a message or a clue to the identity of her killer."

"Unlikely," said Shoop.

"And those other noises," added Pamela, "those aren't human sounds. Some may be sounds of Charlotte or the killer bumping into things as they thrash around during their struggle. But we don't know. If we could identify those sounds--even just one of them--they might lead us to Charlotte's killer."

"Unlikely there too," said Shoop, "Our techs have gone over the inside of that carrel looking for trace evidence, Dr. Barnes. Also, there was no skin found under Dr. Clark's fingernails, so any thrashing she did, didn't produce any trace evidence from the killer."

"Detective," she said, insistently, "that's wonderful, but I was thinking about clues inherent in the sounds on this recording. I don't know what type of forensics analysis your unit will be able to conduct, but I'm trained in acoustics and I'm able to evaluate the sound waves on this recording for a variety of...."

He cut her off mid-sentence. "Dr. Barnes," he said, rising, "I do appreciate you bringing this CD to our attention. We'll definitely investigate it. Rest assured." He stood up behind the desk. She was being dismissed.

"Detective Shoop," she interrupted, remaining seated, "there are a few more things I wanted to tell you. A few things that I-- remembered---and you said I should let you know if there was anything at all that I remembered about the murder or the people connected to Charlotte."

"Yes," he said, sitting back down, and sighing heavily, "what do you remember, Dr. Barnes?"

"First," she began, "I forgot to tell you that the conversation between Dr. Marks and Dr. Clark that I overheard the night of the murder was really more of a fight."

"You heard them?" Shoop asked.

"Yes."

"Do you have any idea what the fight was about?" he asked, jotting this new information in his ever-present notebook.

"Not really," she replied. "Then, the other thing I forgot to mention. This is related. The next day, the day after the murder, our secretary Jane Marie Mira found an envelope in Dr. Marks' mailbox that she believes was put there by Dr. Clark. In it was a photograph of a woman."

"Did she see Dr. Clark put it there?"

"No," she mused, "But, Jane Marie says the envelope was like Dr. Clark's personal stationery. There was nothing in his mailbox when she left and it was there the next morning. And I know for sure that Charlotte was in the main office that night."

"We have only Ms. Mira's word for this," he added.

"Why would Jane Marie make up these things about Charlotte?" Pamela argued, defensively, "Jane Marie was mystified as to who the photograph was. Then, she tracked the photo down from one of the school's yearbooks."

"The photograph that was supposedly placed by Dr. Clark in Dr. Marks's mailbox?"

"Yes," she exclaimed, "The photograph--supposedly--placed by Charlotte in Mitchell's mailbox! Jane Marie found this woman's photograph in a yearbook. She was a student at Grace University about ten years ago, she said. Her name is Evelyn Carrier."

Shoop jotted this information in his notebook too.

"You know, Dr. Barnes," he surmised, "Ms. Mira, your secretary, never mentioned any of this to me when I questioned her the other day."

"I know," said Pamela, sitting up taller, "Jane Marie told me she hadn't thought about it until later. She's actually a bit fearful to say anything about this to you--or anyone. Dr. Marks is her boss. She doesn't want to antagonize him."

"But you can?" he asked, leaning back in his chair and stretching his long legs out over his desk.

"No, but Dr. Marks isn't my immediate superior in the same way that he is Jane Marie's. I assume he didn't mention the fight or the photograph to you."

"Hmmm," mused Shoop, ignoring her question. "Well, is that all, Dr. Barnes? Or do you have any other piece of hearsay or another secret recording you'd like to share?" He stuffed the large cloth back into his pocket. The sound of the humidifier churned away in the corner.

"You know, Detective," she said, "you went to great extremes to encourage me to report to you any little piece of information that I might think of. Now, here I am, bringing you what I consider, some remarkable evidence, and you treat it as inconsequential. At least, I've been able to find something that might help discover Charlotte's killer. Unlike you. It certainly doesn't appear to me that you and your "forensics" team have been able to uncover anything that might lead to a break-through in this case." She stood and was about to leave, her fury increasing by the moment. Her lead foot was itching.

"Sit down, Dr. Barnes," Shoop ordered.

She looked at him and the skeptical, facetious look had disappeared from his face. She slowly lowered herself to the sofa.

"Rest assured, Dr. Barnes," he said with calm intensity, "we are working night and day to find Dr. Clark's killer. I don't belittle any of the information you have provided me. Far from it. I intend to pursue every item. You're not aware of everything we're presently doing to track down the person who killed Dr. Clark, but that doesn't mean that we're not hard at work." He ran his hand through his hair and looked around, as if trying to decide if he should continue. Then he bent over his desk and spoke to her in a whispered voice. "Dr. Barnes, let me enlighten you as to our progress. First, we scoured the lab and Dr. Clark's office for fingerprints, and we're comparing prints taken from Dr. Clark's body with those of all potential suspects. We don't expect to find much there as it appears the killer wore gloves and finger prints from virtually every faculty member are present in the lab. We've searched her office and her home for evidence. Second, we interrogated all individuals who might have seen any suspicious vehicles or persons in or near Blake Hall at the time of the murder. Third, we've interrogated all faculty, staff, and graduate students in your department—in some cases more than once. Fourth, I have, at your suggestion, contacted the subscription database service used by your department and have been able to track down—as of about 45 minutes ago" and he looked at his watch, "the exact site Charlotte Clark was looking at when she was murdered."

"You have?" asked Pamela, now thoroughly engrossed in the man's tale. "What was it?"

"Maybe you can enlighten me on this," he said, almost to himself. "When she was murdered, Dr. Clark was reading an article, a dissertation actually, by a Jonathan Pierce Culver, on your specialty subscription to *Dissertation Abstracts'* full text service. She was on page 87, the cursor highlighting paragraph 5. The dissertation was entitled, "Sexual Dysfunction in Late Adolescence: Addictive Behavior among Young Criminals.""

"It sounds like something she might read for her own work on addiction," responded Pamela. "We do subscribe to *Dissertation*

Abstracts and that extra database you mention does allow us access to the full-text of all registered dissertations."

"So," he said, "you believe that her research the night she was murdered was just something she was working on for one of her own studies?"

"It sounds like it," said Pamela, hesitantly, "yet, I was there Tuesday night, Detective, and I heard how furious she was when she left Dr. Marks' office. I can't see her just storming off to the lab and suddenly changing gears so fast and abruptly working on some of her regular addiction research."

"I agree," he said, tapping his pen. "There's something else." He paused, contemplating, it appeared, if he should share a particular piece of information with Pamela. Finally, he spoke, "We found a small notebook in a locked drawer in Dr. Clark's office desk. In it, there are two columns—one labeled 'source' and one labeled 'copy.' The 'source' column lists names, dates, pages, and lengthy quotes. The 'copy' column lists only quotes and page numbers. There were several different names in the 'source' column, but this Culver was one of them."

"Can I see it?"

Shoop reached into a manila folder on the left side of his desk and pulled out a small three-ring notebook. He handed it to her.

"Any idea what all that means?"

"No," she replied as she perused the small notebook. "It does seem to be related to her research, "but I don't see any reason that she would keep any of her research locked up." She contemplated the various quotes and source citations.

"The fact that this Culver's name appears both in this locked up notebook and on the website she was reading when she was killed," he continued, "tells me there's a good chance that what she was researching online had something to do with why she was killed."

"If it was, why didn't the murderer click out of the site before he or she left?"

"I'd thought of that too," he noted, "but it's possible the murderer just didn't have any time and didn't want to stay there any longer than absolutely necessary. I mean, the killer left the lights on, the door open; he or she left in a real hurry. Is it any surprise, the killer left the computer screen as it was too? Maybe the killer didn't even notice the screen. And, obviously, the killer didn't know about the notebook locked in her desk."

"It's a mystery," she mused. "I'll think about Culver's dissertation, Detective, and the notebook. Maybe something will come to me."

"If it does…"

"I know, contact you right away." She stood up, grabbed her purse, and started for the door. She exited jauntily, leaving Shoop sitting there with a confused look on his face.

Chapter 15

When she pulled into the garage, Pamela had lost most of the bravado that she'd experienced in Shoop's office. Her drive home had not invigorated her; it had depleted her. Now all she felt was desolate. Despite the new evidence about the dissertation that Charlotte was reading when she was murdered and her secret notebook, she still had no greater understanding of the sounds on the CD. It seemed obvious to her that Shoop didn't take the disk and the sounds on it all that seriously. He probably thought it was meaningless. She wondered if he'd even have their forensics' team examine the disk like he said he would. Ha! she thought, "forensics'" team. As if their little police force would have major forensics capabilities. Pamela knew she was far better equipped to analyze the sounds on the disk; she had the experience and the training. If there was any clue to the killer hidden on that disk, she was certain she could discover it.

She opened the kitchen door. The unmistakable aroma of freshly baked bread filled her nostrils. As usual, Rocky was at the stove whistling jauntily. Candide was hanging around at his feet hoping for some morsel to be accidentally dropped. Pamela deposited her belongings on the kitchen table as usual.

"Hey, Babe!" Rocky called out, not missing a beat in his ferocious stirring; something on the stove obviously required his total attention. Pamela was relieved because she didn't want to endure another interrogation—first one from the police, then another from her husband.

"Hey," she said, giving him a quick peck on the cheek.

"Guess what?" he asked, pulling her into his comfy chest. He smelled delightfully like garlic and sausage.

"You've been baking bread."

"Oh, and I thought it would be a surprise," he said, frowning. "I tried a new recipe. Here, take a bite." He shoved the morsel into her mouth.

"Oh, my God," she moaned. "There's nothing like fresh baked bread."

"Technically, a roll," he corrected.

"Roll, schmoll," she said, gobbling down the piece. "Give me more."

"Now, now, don't be greedy. Let's save some for supper. A lovely little sausage soup with an endive salad."

Pamela broke away from his embrace and started towards the bedroom.

"Where's Angie?" he asked.

"Isn't she home yet?" she countered, turning back towards him from the doorway.

"No, she told me when I saw her earlier today that she'd get a ride with you," he said, still stirring.

"She came to my office in the afternoon and I couldn't leave so my graduate assistant Kent offered to take her home," she said. Her trek to the bedroom slowed as she pondered why her daughter still wasn't home hours after she'd left campus. After changing into her comfortable at-home clothes, Pamela returned to the kitchen.

"Kent?" Rocky asked, licking the wooden spoon and holding it out for her to sample, "He's the one who found the...body?"

"Yes, he's very responsible, Rocky," answered Pamela, licking the cheesy soup from the corners of her mouth, and sighing in rapture at her husband's culinary expertise. "They left my office hours ago. I wonder where they could be."

"Maybe he changed his mind and she's stuck over on campus," suggested Rocky, "I mean, why would a graduate student want to be hauling some freshman around?"

"Because she's his boss's daughter."

" Maybe we should get her a car."

"Good Lord," she said, rolling her eyes, "Don't say that in her presence--not even a hint. We'd never hear the end of it."

"I don't like her riding around with some old graduate student."

"He's maybe all of twenty-one."

"No graduate student is that young," he harrumphed.

"They are in Psychology. Only English graduate students are old enough to be grandfathers."

He ignored her jibe and, picking up a spoon, continued stirring his soup. Then, opening the oven door, he reached in with two pot holders and removed another pan of garlic rolls. The aroma was heavenly.

"A nice northern Italian feast, I see," she said, smiling.

"Comfort food," he nodded. "Thought you might like that, after all you've been through the last few days. Did you--you know--take that disk to the police?"

"Yes," she said proudly, puffing out her chest a bit.

"Got to visit your pals at the courthouse," he added teasing

"Yeah, my old buddies at Moving Violations. I hope you're happy."

"Hey, Babe," he shook his head and continued, "It's not a question of making me happy or anyone else. It's just the right thing to do."

"Yeah, yeah," she whined, "I'm Miss Ethical. It's pretty hard to tell students to do the right thing if I don't. I know it."

"Also," he added, "now I feel safer, knowing that it's totally out of your hands and in the hands of the police. Let them deal with this maniac. The further you stay away from it, the better. I worry about you, Babe."

"I know," she said, softly, squeezing him warmly around the waist from behind. "my own private army of one. I really appreciate your concern, but...."

"But?" He pulled away, turning toward her and removing his stirring spoon from the vat of cheese and wine-infused sauce. "What do you mean but?"

"Just that I'll never really be away from it as long as the killer is out there," she said, defensively. "Everyone in the department is in jeopardy until this person is caught."

"But you more so," he concluded, spoon back in pot.

"How so?" she questioned, leaning against the counter.

"Babe, you found the body. The killer doesn't know what you know--or don't know. Maybe the killer had just left when you arrived."

"Kent arrived first. Technically, he would be in greater danger than me."

"Maybe," said Rocky, thoughtfully, "if that's what actually happened."

"What do you mean by that?" she asked.

"You have only this Kent's word for it that he discovered Charlotte when and where he said he did, right?" he questioned, thoughtfully.

"What are you suggesting?"

"I don't know," he said, changing the subject, "I guess I just don't like the idea of him driving around with Angie. Oh, well, that's not the main issue. The main thing is that as far as you're concerned, it's over. The CD is with the police and you can forget all about it, and hopefully things can get back to normal."

"Rocky," she said, seriously, bending in closely to face him directly, "Things will not be back to normal until the killer is caught."

"Yes," he agreed, "But at least you don't have to catch him-- or her."

There was a long pause as Pamela contemplated how to respond to her husband. They did not keep secrets from each other. The few times in the past when she'd tried to keep important information from Rocky, it had ended badly. She always felt better when she confided in him--no matter what the consequences. But, now, she knew that if she told her husband, he wouldn't understand what she knew she had to do. Yet, she could not, in good conscience, keep information from him that could potentially impact her--and thus him--in such a major way.

"Rocky," she began.

"Hmm," he said, listening but concentrating on his dinner preparations.

"I think I should tell you something," she stated.

"What?" he asked, pulling his spoon out of the pot.

"I--I--made a copy of the disk before I took it to the police today," she blurted out in one quick breath.

He slammed the spoon on the counter and turned abruptly towards her, his face becoming red, "You did what?"

"I made a copy of it--so I could study it. I think I might be able to find out some valuable information about the murder--or the killer--if I can just have some time to listen to the recording and do an acoustic evaluation," she said all at once. She stood facing him, defiantly, breathing deeply.

"Are you crazy?" he yelled. "I thought we went through all this! This is dangerous, Pammie! You're putting your life at risk. This maniac has killed one of your colleagues."

"I know, I know," she argued, "But even if the killer knows I have a recording of the murder--which is unlikely--how would my giving it to the police make me any safer? I mean, just the fact that I recorded it would be sufficient reason to make me a threat to the killer--if the killer knew that I had such a disk--and I'm not at all convinced that anyone knows about it--except you, and now Detective Shoop. I just don't see how my keeping a copy places me in any greater danger than my making the original recording in the first place." She felt she'd made an excellent presentation and saw no reason how Rocky could fault her superb reasoning.

"Pammie, anything you do, have, or say that's connected in any way to this murder places you in danger. You're already in danger by being the one--or the second one--to discover the body. You stand out. Anything you do that's different will make the killer consider your behavior. You need to remain discreet--in the background. You can't do anything that looks even the slightest bit suspicious, don't you get that?" He was really getting worked up.

"I'm just fine," she said, firmly. "Why can't you see that? I'm not helpless. I don't need Super Husband to rescue me."

"Babe," he said, grabbing her hands in his, "Whether you want to admit this or not, someone--probably one of your colleagues or one of your students--a person you no doubt see every day--killed someone--and they're desperate and they'll kill again if they feel they're threatened. Right now, you're probably the biggest threat they have. They could be watching you--your every move--whether you realize it or not. They may be scared to death that you'll discover them. You simply can't just go about your business as usual."

"Stop it, Rocky!" she yelled, pulling away from his grasp. "You seem to think I'm a juvenile. I know what I'm doing and I'm being careful. You've got to believe me. I made the copy and I intend to examine it and--if possible--figure out who killed Charlotte. My God, it's the least I can do."

"It's not your job," he pleaded, "Why can't you understand that?"

"It is my job!" she cried, "It's what I do. I listen to sound--human sound--and I figure out what it means. Here's an opportunity for me to take what I do and use it to do something truly meaningful--to avenge Charlotte's murder--and maybe even prevent another murder."

"Even if it's your own?" he asked.

"It won't come to that," she said, suddenly clutching her caring, dear husband close to her body and squeezing him as tightly as she could.

The front door swung open and Angela breezed into the house.

"Hey!" she called from the front entry way, "Where is everybody?"

Pamela and Rocky pulled apart and turned to greet their uncharacteristically cheerful-sounding daughter.

"In the kitchen," called Rocky. He started putting the food into serving bowls.

"Hey, Mom!" said Angela, entering the kitchen and grabbing a garlic roll from the pan.

"Where's Kent?" asked Pamela, "Is he here?"

"He just dropped me off," chattered Angie. She started back down the hallway towards her bedroom.

"Is that all?" asked Rocky, calling after her. "Your mother said you left her office hours ago. Where have you been all this time?"

"Kent showed me the lab—the computer lab--where he works," said Angie, "Then we stopped at Sonic for smoothies. Don't worry, Dad. I'm still hungry. Call me when dinner's ready," and she disappeared into her bedroom.

Kent had showed Angela the computer lab, Pamela noted. She wondered when that had occurred—obviously not when she was there making her duplicate CD.

"The lab?" repeated Rocky, turning to Pamela, "You mean the lab where the murder took place?"

"He works there, Rocky," answered Pamela.

"My God, Pamela," said Rocky through clenched teeth. "You knew she was interested in seeing that place. Why would this guy take a young freshman girl down there to a murder scene?"

"Down there? You make it sound like it's in a dungeon. It's just a computer lab. He's proud of what he does and he loves all that equipment. He's a nice young man."

"And this guy's the one who supposedly discovered Charlotte's body?" questioned Rocky, interrogating her.

"It wasn't supposedly, Rocky," she insisted, "I told you. He did discover her. I was there and I know Kent."

"And you trust him to drive our daughter around and drag her to places where people are killed?" asked Rocky, escorting Pamela to the table, pulling out her chair.

"How many times are we going to go over this? He's very trustworthy; I can vouch for him," she answered, sitting.

"Look, Babe, no twenty-one year old is trustworthy when it comes to teenage girls," said Rocky to her, knowingly. "All right. He may not be a killer, but that doesn't mean I want him anywhere near my daughter." He sat next to her, fuming. Pamela smiled and shook her head.

"You--you—father," she chastised him and laughed. Rocky shrugged and shook his head, seemingly in defeat.

"Angie, dinner!" Rocky called down the hallway towards Angela's room. "Not a word about you-know-what to you-know-whom," he whispered to Pamela.

"I can keep a secret," she whispered back and smiled. That was an understatement, she thought.

Chapter 16

She was nibbling--just nibbling, on another of Rocky's sandwich masterpieces. Every bite she took reminded her of her husband and the mounting number of lies she'd told him--or at least things she'd failed to tell him--in just the last twenty-four hours. It was now just after noon on Friday. The sandwich was a ham and cheese on some sort of Focacchio bread; it was delicious, but she felt guilty eating it. They'd had such a fight last night--and all for nothing. Rocky was mad because he loved her and was concerned for her welfare; she knew that.

But, she just couldn't make him understand her position. Pamela felt a sense of obligation towards Charlotte--not just because she'd found Charlotte's body, but also because she truly believed that the information on the disk might lead to the killer's identity and that she was uniquely qualified to figure it out.

Why did it have to be so hard? Why did doing something she felt was right have to cause this rift between her and her husband? Not just a rift, she thought. No, she'd deceived him— again. She should've never told him she'd made the copy of the disk. She should've just kept her mouth shut. He'd wanted her to dispose of it--then and there--last night. Luckily, she'd thought quickly and told him--lied to him--that the disk was in her office. She'd promised him that she'd destroy it today. Now here she sat, wondering if he sincerely believed that she meant to do it.

Of course, when she'd said all that to him last night, the disk had been in her purse all the time. It was still there now, although she was almost afraid to check. Maybe it had miraculously disappeared and all her worries would be over. Oh, my God, what was she thinking? If it were missing, that would be a catastrophe. Quickly, she reached over, grabbed her purse, and peeked inside. There, in its paper sleeve was the infamous disk--looking thoroughly benign. Taking a deep breath, she put her purse back. Calm down, she told herself, just think this through. She continued nibbling her sandwich.

She couldn't believe this much time had gone by and she still hadn't been able to examine the copied disk. It had been too risky to load it last night at home after what had happened when she'd tried to sneak a glance at the original disk on her home computer. Once she'd gotten Rocky and Angela off to school this morning and straightened up the house (so to speak), it was too late to examine the disk, and she'd had to go to class.

Her morning classes had drifted by as if she were in a hypnotic trance and now here she sat in her office alone for the first time since making the disk. Did she dare listen to the disk here in her office? What if someone came in? She desperately wanted to run it through her acoustic software program to see if there was anything unusual about the sounds on it. Surely, she could close down the program quickly if anyone showed up at her door.

She finished her sandwich and put the wrappings in the brown paper sack which she tossed in her waste basket. Then, taking her cup of tea over to her desk, she angled her monitor so only she could see her screen. Pulling the disk from her purse, she opened the CD drawer and inserted the disk. Pop, click. The computer uploaded the file and Pamela brought up her acoustic analysis program. The spectrograph wave of the two minutes or so of what she believed to be the sound of Charlotte Clark's murder appeared on the screen.

Adjusting the volume knob to the lowest possible level, she placed her cursor at the beginning of the sound wave and pressed play. The ghastly sound of choking floated from her built-in speakers, accompanied by the various bumps, knocks, and clicks. The sounds continued as the cursor flew over the visual output, built to what she would describe as a sort of crescendo, then abruptly ended.

Pamela speculated that Charlotte (or the killer) had inadvertently bumped the "record" toggle switch during their struggle and then bumped it off again as the struggle continued. With this scenario in mind, and placing the cursor back at the beginning of the sound wave, she played it again.

This time, she listened more carefully, stopping the cursor from time to time to replay various segments. She tried to observe the wave visually as she heard each sound auditorially-- connecting sound with wave. Some sounds she recognized as human and some as non-human noises—both by the actual audio produced and the shape of the waves, just as she'd explained to her students in her acoustics seminar the night of the murder. Could it be possible, she wondered, that the killer was making sounds on this tape too, in addition to Charlotte? She moved her cursor back to the beginning of the wave.

Joan Bentley appeared in her doorway.

"Hard at work?" she asked. "Oh, I didn't mean to disturb you. I just wanted to check to see if we're still on for *Who-Who's* tonight? Did you double check with Arliss?"

"God, no!" moaned Pamela, instinctively clicking out of the acoustic program, "I forgot. I got home late, and Rocky and I had a fight."

"Do tell," said Joan, sympathetically.

"I will," said Pamela, "at *Who-Who's*. Let me call Arliss and ask." She called Arliss' extension. Arliss picked up almost immediately. She was obviously talking to some of her creatures.

"Arliss, can you break away from Fluffy and Tuffy," chortled Pamela, "for a few hours tonight to join Joan and me at *Who-Who's*?"

"I was counting on it," replied Arliss, sounding harried, "Stop it, you rascal! Not you, Pam! What time?"

"I tell you what," suggested Pamela, "I'll come down there and get you around five." She looked at Joan, who nodded affirmatively.

"Great!" said Arliss, "You can meet the new rats."

"Meet the rats! Wonderful!" said Pamela, smiling somewhat facetiously for Joan's sake. "See you then."

"I forgot she doesn't have a car," noted Joan. "If you like, since you're bringing her, I'll take her home. *Who-Who's* is so close to where you live, it makes more sense for me to drive her home."

"That would be fine," said Pamela. "I guess that means Arliss never has to be the designated driver."

"I don't mind," said Joan, tapping her forehead, "I can hold my alcohol." She smiled sweetly, waved, and turned to go off down the hall, but turned back.

"I thought you'd be interested to know--and I have this on excellent authority--Rex and Phineas are feuding over first author rights."

"Really?" Pamela looked up, intrigued. "I thought Phineas pretty much did whatever Rex told him."

"Maybe," said Joan, savoring the image, "the little squirrel has found his nuts." She strutted off down the hall.

Pamela thought about *Who-Who's*. There's one interruption I don't mind, she said to herself. If ever I could use a night out with the girls, it's tonight. She took a deep breath and clicked the acoustic program back on, along with turning up the volume control switch. Where was I?, she wondered.

Again, she played the sound wave through from the moment it first appeared until the moment it suddenly disappeared from the screen. Yes, it did seem that someone must have inadvertently bumped the toggle—both in turning it on and in turning it off. The sound appeared to start and end abruptly--as if it began in the middle of a choking that was already taking place and ended in the middle of a choking that was not quite complete. Obviously, thought Pamela, if the choking were complete, Charlotte would be dead and in no condition to either make sound or turn off the toggle switch.

Charlotte must have bumped the toggle on and off during her struggling. It was possible, Pamela mused, that the killer might have bumped it, but she thought not. She thought that since Charlotte was seated, working at the computer, and the killer probably came up behind her, and that that was the position Charlotte was found in, that any bumping of the toggle switch on the computer desk would no doubt have been done by Charlotte. It was probably likely that the killer didn't even realize that the toggle switch was turned on and off during the course of the struggle. If the killer had thought that such a thing might have happened.... She didn't want to even contemplate the ramifications.

Pamela knew that faculty members and students were aware that recordings made in the first row of computers were backed up, but--and it was an important but--did the killer, if the killer was a faculty member or a student, even think of the possibility that a recording might have been made? In the heat of strangling someone, does a killer think of the possibility that the victim might somehow accidentally record the actual murder?

And if so, so what? Here again, Pamela reminded herself that it was not definite that the killer was someone in the department--either student or faculty. It could be, as they had originally thought, some stranger, who entered the lab intending to steal something and Charlotte just got in the way. If that were the case, a stranger wouldn't even be aware of what the lab computers could do.

But Pamela knew one thing; she had a recording of what she was sure was the actual murder, and so far, after dozens of careful listenings, she didn't have a clue as to the identity of the killer.

Chapter 17

Pamela's reverie was interrupted by the ring of the telephone. It was Jane Marie, speaking in an anxious whisper.

"Dr. Barnes," she squeaked. "Are you alone?"

"Yes," replied Pamela, suddenly intent on her receiver. "What's up?"

"I didn't know if I should call you, but I'm worried about Dr. Marks. He's been in his office for almost an hour with the door shut."

"Jane Marie," said Pamela, thinking that Jane Marie's concern was probably misplaced, "that doesn't sound like anything to worry about."

"Yes," she said, "but not after what just happened." Pamela was puzzled. It was not like Jane Marie to cry wolf.

"What just happened?"

"That woman was here," she announced, in her whispered voice.

"What woman?"

"That Evelyn Carrier. You know, the one in the photograph. She showed up several hours ago and asked to see Dr. Marks. When he saw her, he looked startled. He invited her back into his office and I didn't hear a peep out of them for a good hour. I almost called you then, but I was afraid to. Then she left and he went back in his office and closed the door. I'll have to hang up if he comes out."

Pamela was intrigued. The mystery woman had made an appearance.

"When did she leave? Did she say anything?" she quizzed Jane Marie, "What did he say to you? Anything?"

"No, and Dr. Barnes, when she left, I could swear she was crying. Her face was red; her eyes were tear-stained. You know, it looked like she'd been crying. Dr. Marks just sort of said a quick good-bye and then excused himself and shut his door and I haven't heard anything from him since. I tell you, I'm worried. What if this is connected to Dr. Clark's death? I mean, what if--what if--this woman killed Dr. Clark? Do you think she could have threatened Dr. Marks?"

"Jane Marie," said Pamela, in her most reassuring voice, "I think it's highly unlikely that any of this is connected to Dr. Clark's death. If this woman—this Evelyn Carrier were at all involved, I'm sure Dr. Marks would have contacted the police. But, just so you know, I did mention her—and the photo and the big fight--to Detective Shoop yesterday, just in case."

"What did he say?" asked Jane Marie.

"Not surprisingly--nothing," she answered, "I guess that's the detective's motto: ask questions—don't give answers. But, Jane Marie, don't worry about Mitchell. He can take care of himself." Pamela said this, but she herself wasn't totally convinced. She wished she could have seen this Evelyn Carrier or been a fly on the wall during her meeting with Mitchell Marks.

"I've got to go, Dr. Barnes," said Jane Marie, "He may come out any time and I don't want him to catch me gossiping on the phone. I'll see you at the memorial on Sunday, okay?"

"Sure," Pamela answered, but the departmental secretary had already hung up.

Pamela looked at her watch. It was past 4:30 p.m. and if she was going to get Arliss from the animal lab and drive the two of them to *Who-Who's* by five, she'd probably better get going. There was just one thing she wanted to check on her computer before she left. She clicked onto *Google Scholar* and typed in "John Pierce Culver," Nothing. Mr. Culver may have written a dissertation of interest to Charlotte, she thought, but he obviously hadn't produced anything of enough importance to have been picked up by Google's academic search engine. This only meant that Culver never published anything in any reputable journal. So, what was Charlotte doing reading his dissertation the night she was murdered? It was probably not related to her death at all. She closed down her computer and headed out. Joan and Willard had already left, as had most faculty members. It was, after all, late on a Friday afternoon.

Pamela zipped down the corner staircase and onto the main floor. Complete silence. Fridays will do that, she thought. The old building seemed almost haunted, with each of her steps making a creaking noise on the wooden floor boards. Then she saw the lab at the end of the side hallway. Just a brief glance, she thought to herself. This time, as she walked to the lab, she paid close attention to the offices in this wing. She tried to imagine how the killer might have entered the lab, from which direction he--or she--must have come. Had the killer been hiding in an office? The men's restroom was on the other side of the graduate students' office. That's where Willard had said he'd been yesterday when she bumped into him when she exited the lab. The killer could have hidden there and waited until the hallway was clear.

Or maybe the killer had entered from the parking lot? It was a short walk from there to the lab. But if so, how had the killer even known that Charlotte would be there? If, of course, the killer was even looking for Charlotte. So many questions.

She walked quickly towards the lab and unlocked the door. Hardly anyone had even been inside the lab since the murder. Maybe it was because they were frightened. Of course, she--or rather Kent--had cancelled her data collection this week. Next week, there would be more activity. All the more reason to check on things now--when there was little traffic.

As she entered, she flipped on the overhead lights. This time she left the door open. She walked slowly around the lab, looking at all the rows of computers. Was it possible for someone to hide in the lab itself, she wondered? She looked everywhere.

Rocky was right. She was getting herself involved in things she had no business getting involved in. As she quickly left the lab, locking the door, she looked around behind her immediately, almost expecting Willard Swinton to pop up out of nowhere as he had the other day. No one was in sight. This made the third time she'd secretly visited the lab since the murder. Was she tempting fate? Taking too many chances?

As she passed the main office, she noticed the door was closed--and as she pulled it—discovered it was also locked. That meant that Jane Marie had left. It was possible that

Mitchell was still here but, officially, the Department of Psychology was closed for business for the week. She wondered if Mitchell was still in his office brooding about the appearance of the mysterious Evelyn Carrier.

Heading further down the hallway into the opposite wing of the building--where she seldom went--she entered the animal psychology section of her department. She felt a cold shiver--as if someone were watching her. It was no doubt her imagination working over time--or possibly the strangeness of this wing compared to hers. This part of the building was noticeably dirtier and there were sounds of creatures in the distance.

She reached the end of the main hallway, turned left, and continued down the side hallway to the animal lab at the end. The animal lab was in a mirror position to the computer lab--on the other side of the building. It seemed unusual to enter this lab and not see the computers she was so familiar with. As she opened the lab door, she could see Arliss in a white lab coat, with her dilapidated trousers and scuffed up shoes, bent down next to a large cage.

"That's a good fellow, Bailey," Arliss said, coaxing a large chimpanzee. "Hey, Pam!" she called to her friend. "Come meet my buddy."

Pamela strode quickly to the back of the lab. She was not all that taken with animals--her poodle, yes--other animals--not so much. But she feigned enthusiasm because she really liked Arliss, and Arliss was a genuine animal lover.

"Ready to go?" she asked "It's almost five and Joan will probably beat us."

"Yep," nodded Arliss, checking a clipboard that was hanging from the side of the cage. "Hey, there bud, be a pal and let me have a night out with my friends." The chimp whimpered and pulled pitifully on her lab coat.

"Ohhh," said Pamela, sadly. "He doesn't want you to leave." This was another reason she avoided animals. She was a sucker for a sad face and this chimp had a really sad face.

"He's fine," announced Arliss, standing and whipping off her lab coat as she grabbed her back pack from a lab table. "Let's go party!"

Pamela headed out the lab door, with Arliss loping behind. Arliss locked up behind herself and the two women strode down the main hallway of Blake Hall, laughing and talking.

"Just thought you'd like to know," said Pamela to Arliss, "Since I'm bringing you, Joan will be taking you home--as she's closer to you, and *Who-Who's* is closer to me."

"Limousine service!" chuckled Arliss.

"And don't you forget it," said Pamela, shaking her finger at Arliss. "Joan and I expect some payback."

"I'm a great dog-sitter," announced Arliss, "and I know you have a super little poodle, don't you?" Pamela knew that Arliss lived alone in an apartment complex where no pets were allowed; it was probably torture for her, loving "critters" the way she did. They exited Blake Hall and into the small parking lot. Pamela unlocked her car and she and Arliss slid inside.

"Believe me," confided Pamela, "the poodle doesn't need sitting. It's the teenager that needs sitting. Do you want to try your hand at that?" She shook her head hopelessly.

"The perils of motherhood," bemoaned Arliss in a mock serious voice.

"The joys of being single," intoned Pamela. "Believe me, animals are much easier to raise than children."

They were laughing and chatting and having an otherwise relaxing Friday night out. Pamela pulled carefully out of the parking lot—after all, she did have a passenger. They didn't notice the person sitting in a nearby car, watching their every move.

Chapter 18

Joan was already holding court in their favorite booth at *Who-Who's* when Arliss scooted in beside her, and Pamela took up her position on the other side of the table. The cheerful Latin American rhythms pulsating through the sound system and the colorful maracas decorating the walls provided just the ambiance the three women needed to begin unwinding from probably one of the most harrowing weeks their department had ever experienced.

"Did you order?" Pamela asked Joan, removing her jacket and noticeably relaxing. Arliss stowed her backpack under the table and leaned her lanky body across it.

"What!" declared Joan, "You don't trust me to order for you?"

Just then a waiter arrived with three frosty large inverted bell-shaped glasses, each with a lemon wedge neatly upended over the side. He started placing the drinks on the table.

"Margaritas for all!" sang Joan. "My treat!"

"You ladies are celebrating?" asked the efficient waiter.

"No, dear boy," Joan replied, her flirtatious eyes scanning the man's torso quickly up and down. She took a cleansing sip of her Margarita and said, "we're in mourning." She lifted the glass in the air and swung her hips from side to side.

"Joan," grimaced Pamela. The waiter looked confused, but handed each woman a napkin and then took his leave. "You are bad," added Pamela.

"If we're in mourning," asked Arliss, joining in the game. "Then this is the wake, right?"

"Now, you've got the spirit," said Joan, nudging Arliss lightly on the shoulder. Pamela shook her head. Her two friends were angels to try to cheer her up and make her forget the trauma she'd been through. She resolved to put the events of the last few days out of her mind and enjoy herself.

"Hear! Hear!" she saluted them. "Bottoms up!" All three women gulped their drinks. "To Charlotte!" she offered, lifting her glass again. They all clicked their glasses together.

"To Charlotte!" said Arliss, joining in.

"To Charlotte!" added Joan, "wherever she may be!" Then she raised her eyebrows quickly up and down knowingly and they all laughed.

"We're terrible," said Pamela, laughing in spite of herself.

"We'll be the pictures of decorum at the official memorial on Sunday," contributed Joan.

Suddenly, Pamela set her glass down and looked at her friends. "I don't know if I can do this," she said, tears welling up in her eyes.

"Do what?" asked Joan, soothingly, "Have a drink with two good friends? Come, come, my dear." She set down her drink and placed her hand over Pamela's.

"Pam," added Arliss, "we're just trying to cheer you up. I'm sorry if we're making you uncomfortable."

"It's not you," she spoke to Arliss, "or you," she turned to Joan, "but since I found her-her--in the lab--I just haven't been able to think of anything else."

"I know," agreed Arliss, "God, I don't know what I'd have done. I sure didn't like the woman, but I never imagined anyone would kill her."

"Me neither," agreed Pam.

"It doesn't surprise me," said Joan. "That woman was more than just annoying. Maybe you two weren't aware of all her machinations--but, believe me, I've been at Grace University a lot longer than either of you, and I know things you don't."

"Such as?" asked Arliss.

"Let's just say that over the years, Charlotte Clark has been instrumental in the demise of more than one academic career," admitted Joan.

"You don't mean in our department?" asked Pamela.

"My dear," continued Joan, "I've served on many committees with that woman--student thesis committees, service committees, nationally appointed committees, all sorts--and she had her way of getting what she wanted. If she couldn't get it above board, she was not beneath using underhanded methods."

"Why haven't I ever heard about this?" asked Pamela.

"Or me?" chimed in Arliss.

"The woman," explained Joan, "was a master at covering her tracks. To tell the truth, I wouldn't be surprised if some--if not all--of her grants were secured through devious means."

"Such as?" wondered Arliss, turning insistently towards Joan in the booth.

"Such as blackmail," said Joan, suggestively.

"Joan," laughed Pamela, "you must be kidding. Surely, those grant proposals were scrutinized from here to Sunday. How could Charlotte possibly blackmail someone for grant money?"

"I don't know the specifics," explained Joan, "that's why I never would have said anything. And, Lord knows, our department benefited so much from her grants that it would be like cutting off my nose to spite my face to question them." Joan's eye brows rose to hairline height and her upper lip jutted out like a sudden overbite. She returned to her drink.

The women sipped their drinks and sighed, and thought.

"So?" said Joan, breaking the ice, "The most important question."

"What?" asked Arliss, leaning in to her.

"Do you think Mitchell will still go ahead with the Chili Cook-Off?" she wondered aloud. The other two women broke up laughing.

"Maybe we can talk him out of it," suggested Arliss, "in deference to Charlotte, of course." She lowered her head in mock sympathy.

"No," provided Pamela with a new twist, "we must go ahead with the Cook-Off---in honor of Charlotte. We should call it the Charlotte Clark Memorial Chili Cook-Off! Seeing as how Charlotte loved the cook-off so much!" The other two women were laughing uproariously. Arliss was pounding her fist on the leather seat in their booth.

"As Charlotte told us--in private--you recall--so many times!" Joan was elaborating, "She simply loved chili!"

"Yes," agreed Arliss, "If the three of us go in to Mitchell and present this idea, I'm sure he'd go along! I mean you know how much he admired Charlotte!"

"So much!"

"He adored her!" They were cackling now--the margaritas obviously doing their work.

The waiter returned and the women placed their dinner orders. The mood subsided somewhat.

"Really, Pam," said Arliss, "how are you doing? And please don't say 'fine.' It's me--and Joan. You can talk to us."

"I know," she said, finally feeling relaxed enough to speak. "I'm glad I have both of you here. There are some things I'd like to talk to you about. However, most everything I want to say must--I mean must--remain between us three. When I tell you, you'll see why."

"Of course, my dear," said Joan, warmly, "You feel free to tell us whatever you want--or don't want, whatever you need to do. All we want to do is help you cope."

"Right," agreed Arliss, "just help you cope, Pam." The two women looked at her keenly. Pamela took a deep breath.

"I think you know," she began, "what happened when we--I mean—when my grad assistant Kent and I found Charlotte. You don't know some other things--things I haven't discussed but need to discuss. Maybe I shouldn't discuss." She bit her lower lip.

"My lips are sealed," said Arliss, performing the locked key gesture with her fingers in front of her lips.

"Mine too," mimicked Joan.

"First," started Pamela, "yesterday, after the police had finished examining the lab and we were free to go back in, I went down there and looked around."

"Did you find a clue?" asked Arliss, excited.

"Sort of," said Pamela, "but not the way you mean. I was looking at the booths in the front row where Charlotte was strangled--you know, Joan, how the control panel is configured there."

"Vaguely," answered Joan, "I really don't pay much attention to it, since I don't ever use it in my research."

"I don't know if you've ever noticed it before," continued Pamela, "but the toggle switch on the first row computers—is on the right, placed about where your elbow might rest if you were seated there with your arms stretched out. As you know, the master console panel makes back-up recordings of anything recorded by any computer in the first row."

"Again," said Joan, "I never use that function, so I really don't pay much attention to it."

"That's what happens," said Pamela, "So, if the toggle switch is bumped accidentally, a back-up recording would be made, even if the person sitting at the computer did not intend to record."

"My God," said Arliss, her mouth open, "I think I know where this is going."

"Then tell me," added Joan, "because I'm in the dark."

"What if?" questioned Pamela, "What if Charlotte had accidentally bumped the toggle while she was being strangled?"

"Wouldn't the police have seen it and downloaded it?" asked Joan.

"Not if she then accidentally turned off the toggle switch while she was thrashing around," contributed Pamela.

"Wouldn't the killer see what was happening?" asked Arliss.

"If you were strangling someone, would you be concerned about whether or not their elbow accidentally bumped a toggle switch?" queried Pamela.

"I suppose not," said Arliss, thoughtfully.

"Anyway," continued Pamela, "on the off-chance that Charlotte had accidentally bumped the toggle switch on and then maybe off, I went to the back-up storage in the master control console and brought up all data recorded for the first row of computers on Tuesday and guess what?"

"My God," said Arliss, her mouth even wider now. "You found it!"

"Yes," confirmed Pamela, "For a brief period of about two minutes on Tuesday night, a back-up recording was made in Carrel #4--the carrel where Charlotte was found dead."

"Did you listen to it?" asked Joan, with great anticipation.

"I did," she answered.

"And?"

"There is a recording of what sounds like a person choking and various other bumps, slams, clicks, knocks--non-human sounds," she declared.

"Pam," said Arliss, "What I don't understand, is, what good does it do to have a recording of Charlotte being strangled? Does she say who the killer is? Does she give any hint at all?"

"No," said Pamela, deflated, "you wouldn't expect it to be that simple, would you?"

"So, let me get this straight," said Joan, carefully, "you have a recording of Charlotte being murdered, but it doesn't really help us find the killer."

"Us?" exclaimed Arliss, aghast. "What us?   This isn't something we--or Pam--should be involved in."

"And," Pamela quickly added, "I took the recording to the police the next day."

"That's good," said Arliss. "Maybe they can find something in it that will help find the killer."

"I doubt it," mused Pamela, looking pensive.

"Why?" asked Arliss.

"Really," said Pamela, "not to sound conceited, but I do have extensive experience in analyzing sound waves--human and non-human.   If anyone can make sense of the sound on that recording, it should be me."

"Pamela," said Joan, intending to be the voice of reason, "this is not a matter of who has the most expertise. This is a matter of safety."

"Joan," moaned Pamela, "now you sound like Rocky."

"Please don't say I sound like that big, soldier boy of yours!" she shrieked.

"Not your voice, your complaint."

"Joan is right," chimed in Arliss, "I'm so glad you don't have that recording. I mean if it got out that you did, the killer—whoever he or she is--might target you. Oh, God, Pam."

"Then," she sighed.   "I guess you'll have to keep on worrying."

"I thought you said you gave it to the police."

"Not before I made a copy for myself," she answered, reaching down under the table, into her purse and bringing out the notorious disk, showing them a glimpse of it, then quickly returning it to her purse. "Look, I found Charlotte. I feel a sense of responsibility for what happened to her. I know I can find something in that recording if I just have enough time to work on it."

"I think," said Joan, shaking her head, "that it's very unwise. I think you're simply asking for trouble, my dear."

Their dinners arrived and for a while there was silence as the three colleagues scarfed up their enchiladas, burritos, and tortillas--along with buckets of salsa and chips.

"Yum," intoned Pamela, "Wonderful!"

"How does this compare to what that gourmet general of yours makes?" asked Joan.

"Different," she answered, "It's nice for a change. And, of course, the company cannot be beat." She smiled at her two friends who returned her warm expression.

"Pam," said Arliss, slowing down on her enchiladas, "Didn't you say you had several things to tell us?"

"I did," she replied.

"You mean, there's more than--" Joan bent in close, and whispered, pointing discreetly to the disk under the table, "the audio recording of the actual killing that could get you killed?"

"This is probably not so dramatic," she tossed out, "just more like some juicy gossip, which you may already have heard."

"Speak! Speak!" said Arliss, encouraging with hand gestures, hot sauce dripping out of her mouth.

"I have this in confidence from Jane Marie, so you have her to thank for it, but, please, don't accredit it to her--you might get her in trouble,"

"Jane Marie who?" asked Arliss, shrugging.

"Don't know the woman," agreed Joan, munching a tortilla chip.

"The night of the murder, right before my seminar, Charlotte and Mitchell had a horrible row in his office—I heard them."

"Do you know what it was about?" asked Arliss.

"Not really," said Pamela, shaking her head, "just that it was loud. Then, here's a follow-up. The next day, Jane Marie found an unaddressed envelope in Mitchell's mailbox that was not there the night before when Jane Marie left. Jane Marie suspected it was from Charlotte because she recognized Charlotte's personal stationery. She opened the envelope and discovered a photograph of a woman."

"A photograph of whom?" asked Joan.

"Jane Marie didn't know," said Pamela, "There was just a photo. No note. She had no idea who it was, but she thought it might be a former student and so she went through some old yearbooks and found this woman's picture in an annual from about ten years ago. Her name is Evelyn Carrier."

"That's weird," said Arliss, "Why would Charlotte put a former student's photo in Mitchell's box without a note?"

"Yes," agreed Pamela, "why? Anyway, there's more. This afternoon, the woman shows up and asks to see Mitchell. She goes in his office and stays there for about an hour. All this according to Jane Marie. When this Evelyn left Mitchell's office, she was traumatized, said Jane Marie. She'd been crying and her eyes were bloodshot."

"Maybe," suggested Arliss, "she didn't know about Charlotte's death, and Mitchell told her. She could have been one of Charlotte's former students or something."

"Yes," said Pamela, "that's possible, but why the subterfuge on Charlotte's part? Why not just give him the photo? Why not attach a note? Why put just a photo in his mailbox with nothing attached? And why would Mitchell keep that from Jane Marie? He tells her everything. He hasn't said a word to her about any of this."

"It's a mystery," said Joan, looking puzzled. "Do you think it's connected to Charlotte's murder?"

"I don't know. Maybe," said Pamela.

"It does seem like a possibility," said Arliss. She took a deep breath. "Do you think, whatever it is, that it was so horrible that it gave Mitchell a motive to murder Charlotte?"

"Mitchell murder Charlotte," said Joan. "That's ridiculous. They may have yelled at each other, but he's Casper Milktoast; I can't see him physically attacking anyone."

"Joan," said Pamela, "can you see anyone in the department attacking her?"

"No," said Joan, "but if the killer is someone who had a personal grudge against Charlotte, it could be anyone. There must be hundreds of people who fit that bill."

"Maybe it was this Evelyn," suggested Arliss.

"The police seem to think it's someone in the department," suggested Pamela, carefully.

"Why?" asked Arliss.

"First," responded Pamela, "look at access. Anyone in the department could have done it. We all have keys to the lab. Charlotte was alone in the lab; she probably locked the door after herself. Only faculty members and grad students who had checked out lab keys could have gotten in. That limits the pool of suspects quite a bit."

"But the door was open when you found her, you said," argued Joan.

"The killer probably left it open when he—or she—left," responded Pamela, "but that doesn't mean that Charlotte was working in the lab alone at night with the door open. I'm sure she probably locked herself in. She was fanatical about lab security. Remember what Mitchell said at the meeting."

"So," said Arliss, looking worried, "the police really do think the killer is one of us."

"Yes, because we have keys," said Pamela, "I know it wasn't me, and I'm fairly sure it wasn't either of you. So who does that leave?"

"Mitchell, Willard, Rex, Laura, Phin, Jane Marie, and Bob," listed Joan, counting on her fingers.

"It wouldn't be Bob," said Arliss, quickly.

"Dear," answered Joan, "I was just listing the faculty members who didn't happen to be sitting here."

"That does narrow the field, doesn't it?" said Pamela. "But, we know all these people. Truly, I can't imagine any of them killing anyone."

"Maybe the police are wrong, Pamela," said Joan, firmly, "maybe it is someone from the outside."

"And speaking of someone from outside, have either of you ever heard of a researcher named John Pierce Culver? Who did research on addiction?" queried Pamela.

"That would be in Charlotte's domain," answered Arliss.

"Joan?"

"The name doesn't ring a bell. Why do you ask?"

"Because Charlotte was reading his dissertation online when she was killed," responded Pamela. "Shoop told me when I dropped off the disk yesterday."

"So? Does it matter what she was reading?" asked Arliss.

"Normally, I'd say not," answered Pamela, thinking, "but when she left Mitchell's office that night she was in a fury. I just can't see her toddling down to the lab and suddenly focusing on her addiction research. I think there's a possibility she was working on something that led to her murder." She felt a sudden shiver roll up her spine as she realized she hadn't mentioned—and didn't intend to mention to the two women—the secret notebook that Shoop had showed her. "Oh, my," she added, looking at both of their faces, "I've totally monopolized this evening. I haven't even asked either of you about what's going on in your lives."

"My dear," sighed Joan, "what excitement is there for a widow whose children live thousands of miles away? I live vicariously through you."

"And you, Arliss?" asked Pamela, turning to her more laid back friend.

"Same 'ol, same 'ol," shrugged Arliss.

It was getting late. The women had finished their meals--and several Margaritas. Discussing a murder that had recently been committed in their department had had a sobering effect on their behavior. They decided that it was time to go, so they gathered their belongings, divided up the check three ways, and headed out of *Who-Who's*. After farewell hugs, Arliss slid into Joan's car, as Joan had promised, and the two women took off.

Pamela got in her car, switched on her ignition and her headlights, and exited *Who-Who's'* lot onto Jackson Drive toward her home. It was fairly busy for a Friday night, but *Who-Who's* was on her edge of town and wasn't too far from her house. Soon she was in the country, a non-populated area, and the number of cars diminished.

One car behind her was particularly bothersome, its headlights on bright. The driver was, as far as Pamela was concerned, following much too close. How infuriating! She squinted and tried to turn away from the glare shining at her in her rear view mirror. As she looked up, checking, she noticed that the vehicle behind her was getting even closer to her car, as if the driver was trying to annoy her. Should she speed up or would that encourage the driver to chase her? If she slowed down, the driver might take advantage and taunt her.

It was probably some teenage joy rider out on a Friday night, she thought, up to no good. She sped up a bit to test the waters, and the vehicle behind followed suit, getting progressively closer and closer. As she watched the actions of the car in her mirror, she realized that within a few more seconds, the car would slam into her if she didn't do something immediately. She increased her speed. Her turn was coming up quickly. If she could just make it to her turn, maybe by turning onto it abruptly, the vehicle behind her would keep going straight and leave her alone. Here it came, her turn. Quickly she jerked the steering wheel to the right and her car swerved down the side street. The car behind her sped beyond her down Jackson Drive.

Struggling to maintain control of her vehicle, Pamela drove as fast as she could, winding through the streets she knew so well to her home, before the crazed driver could figure out what had happened, turn around, and follow her into her sub-division. She saw her house. Quickly, she pressed her garage door opener, willing the door to open immediately, but it groaned slowing upward. As fast as possible, she drove inside her garage and immediately hit the button to drop the garage door. Only then, did she get out of her car.

Now, she thought, panting with fear, was that a coincidence? Or was someone out to get her?

Chapter 19

Rocky, of course, was waiting for her. When she told him of her encounter with the crazed driver, he became even more incensed than usual, insisting that she call the police immediately. She sat on the edge of their bed, still clutching her purse and books.

"Rocky, no!" she pleaded, "I just need to calm down for a moment. I can't take anymore police right now." She looked at him soulfully.

"All right," he demurred, "but, just until you relax a bit, then we're contacting them."

"Fine," she agreed, and set her belongings aside and removed her jacket. "Is Angie here?"

"No, she's spending the night at Tina's. Did you get anything to eat?" he asked.

"Yes," she responded, "Plenty of *Who-Who's'* burritos and several of their margaritas."

"Are you sure this guy in the car wasn't some alcohol-induced figment of your imagination?"

"Definitely not!" she said, with irritation.

"Okay, Babe," he said, "just wait here a minute. I know what you need."

She leaned back on the bed, her head feeling like a throbbing tomato on the pillow. Oh, my God, she wondered. How much did I drink? I know what I experienced, and I was chased by a crazy driver. It did happen.

Rocky was gone for a while. When he returned, he handed her one of his famous cups of hot cocoa.

"Work on this," he said. She sipped slowly on the luscious liquid, the foam top coating her upper lip. Her husband disappeared into their bathroom and soon she could hear water running in their tub. When he returned later, he grabbed her hand and led her to the bathroom.

"Let's get those clothes off," he ordered.

"Yes, sir!" She gave him a wobbly salute.

She saw that he'd filled the tub and put in her favorite bubble bath. He'd lit a vanilla candle and set it on the sink, the aroma from the wax filling the room. She stripped off her blouse and skirt and then slid out of her underwear. Carefully she lifted a leg over the edge and lowered herself into the tub.

Rocky dimmed the lights until only the flickering candlelight remained. He sat at the end of the tub near her feet and pressed the Jacuzzi button. Immediately soft foam churned into large billows. Sliding lower in the tub, Pamela leaned her head back.

"Give me your foot," he ordered. She lifted her right leg and placed her heel in his palm. Using firm but consistent movements he massaged the bottom of her foot, being careful to manipulate each toe. Pamela experienced relaxation move throughout her body, her worries seeping slowly away, as if passing out of her foot and into Rocky's strong hands.

"So," he spoke softly, "do you feel like talking or should I just rub?"

"Rub," she mumbled.

"You must've had a great time with your girlfriends," he noted, smiling.

"Yup," she agreed.

"The three of you probably were in gossip heaven," he added.

She opened her eyes, somewhat annoyed. "Gossip? Never!" she declared. "We're scientists. We analyze. We evaluate."

"Yeah," he said, nodding perceptively, "It looks like you've analyzed yourself into a drunken stupor. I'm surprised you made it home."

"And with a maniac following me," she added, waving her arms around.

"Well," he observed, "you won't have to worry about that this weekend."

"Why?" she asked, sitting up a bit, the tub water sloshing around.

"Because I called the police when I got your cocoa and told them what had happened," he told her. "I actually spoke with your Detective Shoop."

She realized she should be mad at him for calling Shoop, but she was just too tired.

"My Detective Shoop? He was there working on Friday night?"

"Amazing," he said, "Your local law enforcement hard at work. He seemed reasonable enough--and concerned about you. He said--and these were his words---'I told your wife to lay low.'"

"I was laying low," she protested, "I was having drinks with my friends."

"That's not what he meant," he scolded her, "He was talking about making that damn disk." He rubbed harder on her foot.

"Hey!" she shrieked, "If you're annoyed with me, don't take it out on my toes."

"Sorry, Babe," he apologized. "I only want to help you— really."

"I know, honest," she said, feeling a cold shiver move from her spine through the water. "I don't know if what I'm doing is right or wrong--foolish or smart. I really don't know."

"Then, just don't do anything," he urged, "Let the police do their job. It's their job to investigate murders--not yours."

"But, Rocky," she cried, "I found her. Charlotte was a colleague. No, I wasn't crazy about her--but I found her body. I feel I owe it to her to do what I can to find her killer. And, don't you see? The main clue--if there is a clue in all of this--is sound. Sound. That's my specialty. If anybody in all this mess should be able to figure out the sounds on that recording--it should be me. It's as if fate is telling me to plunge ahead, saying 'You found her body. Now, you find her killer.'"

"You're a crazy woman," said Rocky, shaking his head, "but you're my crazy woman." He gently put down the foot he'd been massaging and reached over and lifted her other foot, and began his ministrations on that appendage. She let him rub her foot and enjoyed anew the tingling sensations on this part of her body. She began to relax again, the bubbly water calming her.

"So, what did Shoop say when you told him about the driver who followed me from the restaurant?" she asked.

"He said there wasn't much they could do." Rocky seemed deflated. "But he did say they'd send a patrol car to drive by our house and check to make certain no one was bothering us."

"That was nice," she answered.

"Yeah," he grumbled, "nice. A murderer follows you home and you say nice."

"Rocky," she repeated, "It was probably just some drunken teenager. It's Friday night, for heaven's sake."

"Anyway," he announced, "you have the entire weekend to relax and take it easy. No thinking about murder."

"Not the entire weekend," she noted, "I have to go to Charlotte's memorial service on Sunday afternoon."

"You'll be getting an escort for that," he said, with a pointed glare, "Me."

"That will be lovely, dear," she smiled back at him. "You won't mind then," she asked, tentatively, "if I listen to the disk, will you?"

"Do I have a choice?"

"No," she said sweetly, rubbing her free foot against the inside of his knee.

"Not fair," he said.

"Anyway," she continued, "I really need to be able to discuss what I hear with you. There is obviously Charlotte's choking. But there are a lot of other odd noises--bumps, scratches, clicks, scrapes. If I could identify some of the noises, maybe I could figure out something about the killer."

"How?" he asked.

"I don't know," she responded. "Maybe one or more of the noises might be connected to someone or something. I just have no idea."

"Yeah, yeah," he nodded, expecting the next remark, "you're a scientist. You have to follow the data."

"Right!"

"I do have some other tidbits for you to savor," she teased.

"As a cook," he noted warmly, "I'm all for savoring."

She told him about the big fight and the mysterious photo and then added, "Oh, and that's not all. There's the Tenure

Committee. We have three candidates up for tenure this year--
but, the Dean apparently wants to restrict our department to
two."

"That hardly seems fair," he mused.

"I know," she added, the bubbles dripping off her shoulders.
"Mitchell was pushing, I think, for Rex and Phineas. Charlotte
was probably behind Laura because she was her protégé."

"Maybe," he suggested, "that was the subject of the big
fight."

"Could be," she noted, "but I can't believe Mitchell would kill
Charlotte because they disagreed over who should get tenure."

"Stranger things have happened," he said, looking
momentarily past her.

"And Shoop told me that they found out that Charlotte was
reading a dissertation on addiction by some guy named Culver
on the computer screen when she was murdered."

"Is that important?"

"I don't know—it could be, but I can't figure it out," she said
biting her lip. "I forgot," she said, gleefully, on her knees now, "I
forgot this in all the craziness. On the night of the murder,
Phineas even stopped me in the hallway and asked about the
possibility of a candidate removing his name from consideration
for tenure."

"Why?"

"I've no idea," she frowned, sliding back down into the water.
"I wish I could figure this all out. And I wish I could figure out
what was on that disk." She tapped her fingers on the edge of
the tub.

"You'd better do whatever you're going to do out of the tub,"
said Rocky, standing and walking over to the door, "or you'll be
a prune in the morning." He grabbed her night clothes from a
hook behind the door and placed them on the sink. Then he
pulled a large terrycloth towel from a rack on the wall. "Here,"
he said, opening the towel, and holding it out for her.

She shimmied off the wayward bubbles and stepped out of
the tub, shaking first one leg, then another. She turned her back
and allowed Rocky to wrap her gently in the warm folds of the
towel. Then he grabbed her night clothes from the back of the
door.

"Everything you need," he said, "nightgown, slippers, robe."

"No," she replied, slowly turning towards him and dropping the towel. "I don't need any of those things." She smiled warmly at her husband and held out her arms.

Chapter 20

Sunday afternoon proved perfect for Charlotte's memorial service.   The weather was clear and brisk.   The venue was lovely, thought Pamela.   The campus chapel was a large red brick edifice with towering white columns and white steps leading up to its imposing entrance.   Oak tree branches hung heavy over the entire building, their multi-colored leaves turning the entire scene into a riot of fall shades.

Pamela had arrived early with Rocky at her elbow. Amazingly, Angie had decided to attend also, when she realized that her chauffeur of the previous day, Kent, would probably be in attendance.   As the trio entered the lobby of the church, Pamela was surprised by the large turnout.   Mitchell was near the door, acting as "official" greeter.   The Dean and other members of the administration milled around, speaking with faculty and potential donors.   Pamela spied Detective Shoop tucked in a corner, dressed in his standard shabby grey suit. If Shoop was here, she speculated, quite likely other police officers were stationed around the chapel discreetly listening to conversations of potential suspects.

Rocky was soon deep in conversation with a colleague from the English Department. Angie found Kent leaning against one of the tall white pillars, and the two of them were quickly embroiled in animated talk.   Kent appeared a bit more dressed up than usual, having donned a purple jacket.   Angie had even gone so far as to put on a dress and flats. Both of them, however, were still arrayed primarily in their standard black.   Pamela noted that they would always be ready for a funeral—at least as far as their clothing was concerned.

Over her shoulder, Pamela glanced down at the other end of the lobby where she could see Joan and Arliss talking to Bob and Willard.   True to his word, Willard was wearing his all black outfit. Joan was bedecked in a subdued flowery suit and Arliss had on a nice pair of gabardine trousers and a simple white silk blouse. She had foregone her standard sneakers for a simple pair of low dark heels. Pamela was unexpectedly surprised; Arliss almost looked feminine. Bob was wearing a nice dark suit with a rich magenta sweater vest. All of her colleagues looked quite presentable, she thought. Too bad it took Charlotte Clark dying to do it. As she strolled over to them, smiling at people along the way, she listened to snippets of conversations from different groups.

She heard two of her graduate students discussing readings that were assigned for one of their classes.

"I just finished it," said one, "I didn't have time to decide whether I liked it or not."

"It didn't take me any time to decide," said the other, "It stank!" They guffawed quietly. Typical of students, always complaining, she thought, about assignments, whether undergraduate or graduate.

"Greetings," she said to her four colleagues, Joan, Arliss, Bob, and Willard, when she reached them. "Arliss, why are you looking so glum?" Arliss did look morose, even annoyed. Maybe it was because she was dressed up—especially wearing heels. She kept shifting from foot to foot as if her shoes were too tight. She looked miserably uncomfortable.

"I'd rather be anywhere other than here," declared Arliss, "Charlotte was not one of my dearest friends." She scowled and kicked her foot.

"Now, dear," said Joan, patting Arliss' back in a comforting manner, "It's only for a brief while and then we can be on our way—and free of Charlotte for good!" Pamela always loved how Joan managed to find something pleasant in the most unpleasant of situations.

"Absolutely," added Willard, "why don't we all go to the Reardon Coffee Factory afterwards?"

"Great idea," chimed in Bob, "I'm game."

"It sounds lovely," said Pamela, "but I have a husband and daughter in tow."

"You brought your burly sergeant-major with you?" questioned Joan, obviously delighted. "Where is he?" She looked around the gathering.

"Off analyzing books with one of his cohorts I suppose," Pamela replied.

"Actually," added Bob, "despite the gravity of the occasion, I'm surprised to see so many faculty here from around campus. It's nice to know that our department has this kind of support."

"Even if it is for Charlotte," snickered Arliss.

"Arliss," said Bob, giving his young assistant an eye roll and an elbow nudge.

"Enough of you, Miss Sourpuss," said Joan to Arliss, tsk-tsking. "Why don't we go get some good seats?"

"Good seats," replied Arliss. "Joan, you sound like we're going to the movies—not a funeral."

"Wherever I'm going, I want to be able to see what's going on. Come on, everyone!" She pulled Arliss' arm and the two women trudged through the entry to the chapel, followed by Willard. Bob remained behind.

"Pamela," he said, "could I have a quick word with you about the upcoming Tenure Committee meeting? I understand that Mitchell has appointed Joan to replace Charlotte."

"Yes," answered Pamela, "he has. What did you want to discuss?"

"You may also have heard that the Dean is pressuring us to select two—not three candidates."

"I had heard that, Bob." From almost everyone.

"I think this cutback in candidates is just the start of some nasty news to come. Look at it this way, the Administration believes--rightly or wrongly--that our department has had more than its fair share of funding lately, and I think they'll try to cut our budget wherever they can. If the Administration gave tenure to all of our candidates—Rex, Phin, and Laura—that would mean that all eligible faculty in our department would have tenure. No other department on campus could say that. If the Administration approved tenure for all three of our candidates, there would be an outcry from other departments who had faculty with terminal degrees who don't have tenure and who've been turned down for tenure more than once."

"You really think so?" She had never considered tenure from this perspective.

"Yes. Of course, I'm hoping that Mitchell will fight for our candidates, but I have to be honest, Pam, I think he's more likely to be considering what the situation means for him. He has tenure and it really doesn't make any difference to him if one of our three candidates is denied."

"Bob," said Pamela, "It never crossed my mind that we'd be forced to decide tenure for our candidates based on anything other than their own individual merit."

"I know," he said. "It makes the University seem just like a business--way too cut-throat for me. It's just another indication of the administration's priorities--certainly not education--or I wouldn't be having the hell of a time I am trying to get even a little funding to keep the animal lab afloat, as you know."

"I know, Bob. I'm so sorry about that and about the way Charlotte treated the animal lab," she sighed. "She was horrible to you."

When she said these words, Pamela was immediately struck with a memory of a recent faculty meeting where Charlotte had verbally attacked Bob in one of her tirades against the animal lab. It had started when Mitchell had informed them that the increased funding they all had expected from the Dean would not be forthcoming:

"No!" Bob had yelled, jumping up, slamming his hands on the table. "Mitchell, you promised you'd fight for us with the Dean. You told me that he knew how serious the situation was in the animal lab and how desperately under-funded we were. I was under the impression that the animal lab was the Dean's highest priority!"

"I know your concerns Bob, and truly, I did plead your case with the Dean, but I'm afraid," Mitchell had replied, trying to avoid looking directly at Goodman, "that the Dean believes— and these are his words, not mine--that the animal lab is more eyesore than necessity. There's simply no way around it, Bob. I'm afraid he's not going to be providing us with additional funds for the animal lab—or any other departmental project--this year. I'm really sorry, Bob."

"What?" yelled Arliss, also standing. "This is scandalous! How does anyone expect us to teach animal psychology with that run-down animal lab?"

"Maybe they don't," suggested Charlotte Clark. "This is just a regional university and our small Psychology department can't be expected to do everything. It's better that we concentrate on one thing and do it well than many things and do them poorly."

"Are you suggesting that we do poor work, Charlotte?" demanded Bob Goodman.

Charlotte smiled, shrugging her shoulders, "Just take a look at what areas of our department *are* being funded, Bob. My work on addiction, of course, Laura's and Joan's studies on educational psychology, Willard's and Pam's work on linguistics, Rex and Phin's stuff on personality. When's the last time any animal research got funded here? Let's face it, agencies want to fund research that relates to people--not animals. Our department is spread too thin as it is. We'd be better off dropping classes and programs related to animal psychology and getting rid of that bottomless money pit you people call an animal laboratory."

"We people!" shouted Bob. "We 'people' are your colleagues, Charlotte!"

"Now, now!" yelled Mitchell Marks, the sweat glistening on his brow. "Can't we have a nice, quiet, professional meeting for once?"

"Not with Charlotte here!" Bob Goodman yelled.

The fury of that encounter still burned in Pamela's mind. Bob's presence now reminded her of it and of Charlotte's ability to goad them all. She pulled herself from her thoughts and continued speaking to Bob: "It makes me feel guilty to use the computer lab at times, Bob. Those of us who have that lab are so lucky compared to you and Arliss over in the animal wing. I swear, I don't know how you and she manage to produce the wonderful research that you do."

"Thank you," Bob said, smiling. "Luckily, our chimp is doing most of that for us. Bailey's amazing. There's not much that little fellow can't do. To tell the truth, I'm beginning to think that he's actually more sensitive than most people.

Wouldn't that be an amazing finding if Arliss and I could confirm it?"

"Absolutely," Pamela gleamed. "Nothing makes my day more than hearing about someone's research success."

"You're unique in that respect, Pam. Arliss is right," he noted. "I just wanted you to be prepared and think about how all this might affect your vote." He turned and started for the lobby.

"Thanks," she said. "You've given me a lot to think about." He took her hand in his and looked into her eyes.

"I'm glad you're part of our department, Pam," he said, holding her hand warmly. "We're lucky to have you."

"You too," she stammered, not quite certain how to take this unexpected compliment from someone she didn't really know all that well. Then he dropped her hand, turned and scurried off down the center aisle of the chapel to join Joan, Arliss, and Willard. Rocky appeared at her side.

"So, what was that handholding going on between you and the string bean?" he queried.

"Don't be jealous, that's just Bob," she laughed, as they entered the chapel. "Your hands are only ones I want to hold." As they started down the aisle, she spied Rex and Phineas, head to head near a side column. She slowed down in order to pick up what she could from their conversation.

"Second author!" Phin said, at least Pamela thought he said.

"Agreement..." she thought she caught Rex saying, but she wasn't sure.

"...promised that on this article..." said Phin.

"... misunderstood..." answered Rex's garbled voice.

Pamela wondered what the argument was about. She remembered that Joan had said the other day that they were arguing about authorship. It was certainly the most agitated she'd ever seen or heard Phineas. He was usually very docile and subservient to Rex, following him around like Rex's personal servant. Even so, both men had excellent publication records and churned out numerous articles in top drawer journals each year. Yes, they often co-authored articles, but as far as she could tell, the first author credits had been shared equally between the men. Why were they arguing over what appeared to be authorship? She had slowed to almost a standstill in hopes of overhearing more of the Rex Tyson-Phineas Ottenback feud.

She felt a hand gently on her back and she jumped and turned. It was Rocky smiling at her.

"You ready to go in and find a seat or do you need to do some more snooping?"

"Rocky!" she huffed, "I'm not snooping!"

"Of course not. Let me go get Angie and we'll go in," he said.

"No," she said, stopping him. "Angie won't want to sit with us. Let's just go in by ourselves," she added as she peered around to see where her daughter had disappeared to. Was she still chatting with Kent? As she continued to look around, Kent and Angie sauntered into view from behind a large column.

Rocky turned to see his daughter, now giggling and smiling broadly (something she hardly ever did in front of her parents) at the conversational quips of the remarkable Kent. Kent obviously enjoyed having such an enthusiastic audience.

"Is that the infamous Kent?" Rocky asked, as he spied his daughter hanging on the every word of the strangely outfitted young man. "He looks like a total weirdo."

"Now, dear," said Pamela, calming him. "Appearances are deceiving. I told you, Kent is a fine young man."

"She obviously prefers her present company to ours," he admitted. "All right. Let's go get this over with." They walked down the center aisle and scooted into a pew directly behind Joan, Arliss, Bob, and Willard. Pamela felt a tap on her back and as she turned she recognized one of her graduate students.

"Dr. B," whispered the girl, "What seminar are you teaching next semester?"

"My goodness, Mary, let me get through this afternoon—this semester. I'm not even certain they have me scheduled to teach a graduate seminar next semester."

"They have to," the young woman whined, "You're the only one who teaches Research Methods other than Dr. Clark, and now that Dr. Clark is—you know—now that she won't be teaching anything, you're the only one to teach Methods!"

"Mary, there are other faculty members who can teach Methods," replied Pamela.

"But, not like you, Dr. Barnes," she said. "Please, say you'll teach it."

"Again," reiterated Pamela, "It's not for me to say. We'll just have to wait and see." With that, she turned firmly back in the pew and looked ahead as the minister entered from the sacristy.

"My god," she sighed quietly to her husband.

"I hope he's listening," whispered Rocky in her ear, "and I hope he's telling you to behave yourself."

At that moment, the chapel's nondenominational minister climbed the few steps to the side lectern. He was dressed in white and gold satin robes and wore a beautiful golden stole around his neck.

"Good afternoon, my university friends—faculty, students, administration, and sponsors. This is a sad occasion as we must say farewell to one of Grace University's most gracious and benevolent patrons."

That, thought Pamela, was laying it on a little thick. But then, the minister was playing to some potentially big donors in the congregation.

"Charlotte Clark was a legend at this school," continued the preacher, "not only in her own department, but throughout the entire campus. Her fame was worldwide. Her academic credentials were impeccable. Her life was devoted to Grace University. But Dr. Clark's wonderful contributions—and those we know she would continue to make in the future—have been cut short—cut short by an untimely death. Dr. Clark was not the victim of some horrible disease or accident. No, she was taken from us in her prime by a murderer—someone motivated by selfish and personal goals, someone totally unconcerned by the good works that this amazing woman might have accomplished if she had been allowed to live a full and productive life. Now we will never know what feats Charlotte Clark might have done, because she will never get the chance to do them."

Pamela twisted in her seat. Was this man describing the Charlotte she knew? She glanced over her shoulder at the assembled congregation. She could see Shoop now standing at the back of the chapel. Several men—obviously police officers were standing in the side aisles near the back of the chapel. They were all keeping a close watch on the behavior and reactions of the members of the congregation—particularly those who were faculty, students, or staff in the Psychology Department. Did they plan on making an arrest during the service? She hoped not. Besides, who would it be? She doubted they had any inkling yet who could have possibly killed Charlotte. She looked around surreptitiously at the people assembled. Mitchell was in the front row with his wife Velma by his side. Jane Marie and her husband were seated in the same pew. Laura and her husband Vittorio were also near the front. Phin and Rex were seated together in a side pew, although they didn't appear too happy with each other. Neither of their wives had evidently accompanied them. Arliss, Joan, Bob, and Willard—all single--sat together in the pew directly in front of Pamela and her husband in a middle pew.

"Charlotte Clark," continued the reverend, "was devoted to learning the secrets of the horrific scourge of addiction—addiction that robs the body, the mind, and the soul of so many poor helpless victims. Why would anyone take such a patron from the earth?"

He makes her sound like Mother Theresa, thought Pamela. Where, she wondered suddenly, was Angie? She discreetly looked over her shoulder again and spied her daughter sitting next to Kent in a pew near the back of the chapel—where most of the graduate students were seated. As she secretly watched her daughter, she noticed Shoop fanning his gaze over the entire assembly—watching, it appeared, for any tell-tale responses to statements made during Charlotte's memorial. As she stared at him, his glance fell on hers and their eyes met. "Behave yourself, Dr. Barnes," they seemed to say. Pamela felt his scrutiny and turned back in her seat.

"I should note," the minister continued, "that our University President (who could not be here today) has set up a Charlotte Clark Memorial Fund, the proceeds of which will go to a scholarship for a deserving graduate student in Psychology, Charlotte's department. I hope you—Charlotte's friends and colleagues—will give serious consideration to making a generous donation to this important scholarship fund."

Pamela leaned over to Rocky and whispered, "Ah, now I see, it all boils down to money, right?"

"Doesn't everything, Babe?" whispered Rocky.

With that, the minister, opened the Bible on his lectern and offered a short prayer. When he was finished, he announced, "Several of Charlotte Clark's colleagues and friends have expressed a desire to speak. First, I'd like to introduce, Dr. Mitchell Marks, Chair of the Psychology Department." The minister backed down the raised lectern and Mitchell climbed up and adjusted the microphone.

"Friends," he said, gulping a bit, obviously somewhat nervous, "This is a truly sad occasion. Charlotte and I had our differences, but I always remained an admirer of her intelligence, talent, and initiative. She was, without doubt, the star of our department. I don't think I'm stepping on any toes by saying that." He looked out at the see of faces and chuckled a bit. "I know that because I know how much the Psychology Department benefited by having Charlotte as a member. She single-handedly remade our department. Through her funding efforts, we were able to build an amazing state-of-the-art computer lab that has allowed our faculty and graduate students to produce top-notch research. Her generosity was always present and she shared her good fortune with her colleagues. I truly don't know what we'll do without her. That's all, I guess." He coughed a few times and then stepped down carefully, looking somewhat bereft.

"That's it?" questioned Rocky. "He's the head of your department?"

"He is," Pamela replied.

"He's not very good at giving eulogies, is he?"

The minister then introduced Dr. Laura Delmondo. From her seat further back in the crowd, looking cautious and shy, Laura Delmondo passed Mitchell as she walked carefully forward and assumed the lectern. Mitchell nodded towards her sadly as they crossed paths.

"Hello," said Laura, looking more at her note cards than the congregation, "I asked Dr. Marks if I could speak today. I know you all know about Charlotte's amazing academic successes and remarkable generosity. What you may not know is her more personal side." She looked up and stared at the audience for a second and then quickly returned to her cards, " I'd like to change that. I first met Charlotte Clark when I was an undergraduate student here at Grace many years ago. I planned to take a few Psychology classes, get a degree—it didn't really matter in what, get some sort of job for a few years, and then get married and begin what I assumed would be my real life. Meeting Charlotte changed all that. She spoke in class and I suddenly realized that here was a woman with an amazing job—who apparently wasn't married with a family. When I went in to her office one day to speak to her about my research paper, she suggested that I might find a career in Psychology interesting. She said she had read some of my earlier papers and thought I showed promise. The thought of having a career, any career, let alone one in Psychology, never entered my mind. After that, I visited her office frequently and she encouraged me. She helped me get accepted into a graduate program and she pushed me to go on for my doctorate. No one in my family had ever gone to college—let alone had a graduate degree. She changed my life. She opened a new world for me. Yes, along the way, we disagreed, but she was instrumental in me coming here to Grace University to work in the Psychology Department—a place I love and a job I adore. She was responsible for turning my life around. I can't believe she's gone—I can't believe---" She looked out at the crowd again, tears filling her eyes.

Arliss bent her head towards Joan and whispered, "For God's sake, she makes Charlotte sound like her guardian angel." Pamela could hear the annoyance in her voice. Charlotte didn't do any of those things because she cared about Laura. Arliss continued, "She did everything she did for herself. She helped Laura start her career so Laura could become her disciple—her acolyte. So she could worship at the Charlotte Clark shrine."

Arliss stopped her anti-Charlotte commentary when suddenly Laura cried out, "Oh, Charlotte, I'm so sorry!" and burst out crying, running down the center aisle and out the front of the chapel. Her husband quickly followed her out of the chapel.

Pamela sat in stunned silence for a moment as did the rest of the congregation.

Quickly, the minister returned to the lectern and concluded the service with a short prayer. The congregation slowly rose and began exiting the chapel.

"Quite a tear jerker," noted Willard as they all exited.

"Should be good for a few bucks," observed Arliss, as she glanced around at the faces of the potential big donors in the crowd.

"I thought it was a lovely tribute," added Joan.

"Why was that woman apologizing to Charlotte?" whispered Rocky to Pamela. "Do you think she killed her?"

"No, of course not." At least, I don't think so, she thought.

Pamela navigated Rocky through the crowd and outside of the chapel, where finally she felt she could breathe. She wanted to go find Laura and talk to her, but she could feel Shoop's eyes on her back. There would be no more sleuthing for her today.

Chapter 21

Pamela had spent most of the weekend—when she wasn't at the memorial or romancing her husband--listening to the recording of the murder and the sounds of Charlotte choking. Oh, she did manage to get the family laundry done and she attempted to vacuum the living room rug (with "attempted" being the key word), but her focus was on the recording of the murder. She felt certain that Charlotte was not saying--or trying to say—the killer's name or anything else. If she had been, that would really have been unusual. Charlotte was just struggling to breathe. The sounds—or rather, the noises--that were overlaid onto Charlotte's strangled voice, however, were another story.

Pamela guessed that those sounds were probably comprised mostly of Charlotte bumping and scraping things on the computer desk, but she couldn't be sure. Even if she could identify the sounds, what good did it do? Identifying the sounds didn't tell her who the killer was. She felt totally stymied.

When Monday morning arrived, she headed to campus feeling depressed and disappointed with her efforts. After her morning classes, she worked some more on analyzing the recording, but made little headway. Over and over again, she played the recording--Charlotte's strangled choking, the myriad of bumps, clicks, scrapes, and scratches that were probably made by Charlotte fighting for her life. How was any of this helping her? Shoop was right, she realized in frustration; this was a job for the police.

She stopped briefly at noon and gobbled down her regular lunch of sandwich and tea, clicking out of her acoustic software program when anyone came within a few yards of her office door. She kept the volume on her speakers low so the repeated sounds of Charlotte choking were not audible to hallway strollers. Anyone entering her office would assume she was working on her research--which, in a way, she was.

Several students came in during the early afternoon to discuss topics for their class papers and projects. She was even happy for the interruption, because it was obvious that she wasn't getting anywhere with identifying the noises on the disk.

As the time neared three o'clock, students started gathering outside the large lecture classroom next to her office which was directly above the computer lab on the main floor, waiting for Rex Tyson's Introduction to Psychology class. Pamela usually tried to get out of her office before this time, because Rex had two mass lectures back to back on Monday and the noise usually got to be too much for her. Often, she'd go downstairs to the lab and work in one of the carrels when it was clear that no more students were going to show up for her office hours. She always left a note on her door saying where she was just in case. Why not, she thought. I have every reason to go down there and work.

Grabbing the disk from the drawer in her computer, she locked her office door and headed downstairs to the lab. As she expected, Kent was at the check-in desk, signing in the new participants for her study that he'd rescheduled from last week.

"Hi, Kent," she greeted him, "I'm just going to do some work in the computer databases." And I'd really like to know, she thought, if you plan to be romancing my 18-year-old daughter or were the events of last week all my imagination? No. She determined to keep her concerns about Angela to herself.

"Sure, thing, Dr. B," he responded, and went back to the line of subjects signing in. None of them seemed to be particularly upset by being in a lab where a murder had recently taken place.

Pamela went to the first row of computers. She went to Carrel #3, immediately next to the infamous Carrel # 4. Pulling out the wheeled desk chair, she sat down, as close to the spot where Charlotte Clark had lost her life as she could be and still be able to use the terminal, seeing as how all the equipment in Carrel #4 was still missing.

She looked around. What could Charlotte see from here? As she looked around her, she imagined what she would or wouldn't notice if she were Charlotte and were totally involved in her computer research. Charlotte was looking at Culver's dissertation in the subscription database for something--she wondered what. Did she hear the killer enter?

Pamela noticed the sounds of Kent talking to the students at the check-in desk. The acoustic panels in the carrel did an excellent job of muffling the sound. Oh, she realized that people were talking, but she thought it would be quite possible that a person working intently at this computer wouldn't notice someone entering the lab and quietly closing the door. They probably wouldn't even notice the sound of someone walking up behind them. Indeed, the student participants walking to their stations in the second through fourth rows were almost inaudible to her as she sat surrounded by the carrel walls.

Placing the disk in its slot and putting on headphones to muffle the sounds of Charlotte's murder from the students in the lab, she hit play. Would she ever get used to Charlotte's tortured cry? As each noise appeared, she tried to imagine exactly what might have caused it--experimenting with knocking her elbow against the carrel wall to recreate the bumping noise on the tape, dragging her fingernails down the acoustic wall panels to recreate the scraping sounds. She tried many different defensive behaviors within the booth that she guessed Charlotte might have tried that would have resulted in the sounds that she heard on the tape. In all, she believed she'd been able to recreate reasonable facsimiles of all the sounds and thus, account for all the sounds, with the exception of one.

One sound still seemed to have no apparent source within the booth--no source that Pamela felt could possibly have been made by Charlotte as she fought for her life. It was that strange double clicking noise. Click-click. Then a long pause. Then click-click again. Whatever it was, the two clicks seemed to belong together. Whatever prompted one click, also produced the second click.

Possibly, she hypothesized, the clicking noise was not created by something Charlotte did to protect herself. What if, just if, the clicking noise was created by the killer? Maybe not intentionally, but could it possibly be some noise the killer made inadvertently while he/she was in the midst of killing Charlotte Clark? If so, what might it be? What sound would a person make while killing someone? It was obviously mechanical, not human.

Pamela closed her eyes and imagined the killer coming up behind her. She envisioned the killer's hands on her neck, wrapping the power cord of the headphones around her neck and pulling it tight. She'd fight, she was sure. She'd struggle. At this point, Pamela tried to emulate the behavior that she thought Charlotte would have exhibited. Then, she imagined the killer struggling back, maybe pushing Charlotte down, maybe pulling her upwards. Their bodies might be in close proximity. What if? What if something on the killer's body made that noise-- accidentally--when the killer pushed or pulled Charlotte against him or her while strangling her? Whatever the something was-- could it have made such a clicking noise? Surely, the killer wouldn't stop strangling Charlotte to intentionally click this thing. Whatever it was, the clicking noise must have been produced accidentally. But what was it? She felt she was on the right track, but she just didn't know where to go next.

Believing she had exhausted all the possibilities of her laboratory mini-experiment, she popped out the disk and left the lab, waving good-bye to Kent. All of a sudden, she had another experiment in mind that she intended to try--tomorrow. With a few preparations at home, she'd be ready. Yes, tomorrow it was.

Chapter 22

The next day, Tuesday morning, when Pamela entered the building, she carried a mini-tape recorder in her jacket pocket. When she encountered a suspicious sound, she intended to record it secretly and then label it when she had a chance, in her own voice--giving the name and source of the sound she'd just captured. At least, that was the plan.

As she opened the side door of Blake Hall near the parking lot, she clicked the record button on her unseen recorder in order to capture the sound of the door hinges squeaking. It was really just a test of her secret recording skill; she didn't actually think the entrance door was the clicking sound on the disk.

"Blake Hall, front door hinges," she whispered into the lavaliere microphone she had pinned underneath her jacket lapel. Her unseen hand in her pocket switched the off button as she headed down the hallway towards the main office. As she passed people swarming around, she listened for sounds.

Laura Delmondo was coming towards her from the office, balancing delicately on a pair of torturously high heels which made a metallic clicking on the linoleum floor. Pamela pushed the record button in her pocket as Laura's heels tapped against the floor. Was this sound a match to the clicks on her disk? She couldn't tell. Could the mysterious double-click noise be the sound of someone's shoes hitting the floor? It didn't make sense, she reflected, but she made the recording of Laura's shoes and her unseen finger pressed the record button off right after she added her whispered vocal label "Delmondo, shoes" into her shoulder. Laura passed by her with a quick greeting. She didn't really suspect her, but Laura did admit herself to having a fight with Charlotte shortly before her murder and she did have that emotional break-down during the memorial on Sunday. Charlotte wanted Laura to concentrate on research and Laura wanted to work on starting a family. Was that sufficient motivation to kill someone?

Entering the main office, Pamela bumped into Phineas Ottenback getting his mail.

"Dr. Barnes," he mumbled, softly. "So sorry, didn't see you." He pulled a ballpoint pen out of his shirt pocket and began repeatedly pushing the clicker, she noticed, almost like a tic, all the while smiling constantly. As usual, strands of greasy hair dangled over his forehead.

A pen clicking, she thought. Now, that would work. A pen could click even if it were in his pocket if something (like a body) were pushed against it. She quickly pressed her hidden record button. Was this the clicking sound? She'd never paid much attention to Phineas, but he did seem to be full of nervous mannerisms. Maybe he killed Charlotte and then quickly picked up his pen and started punching it because he was so upset. Or possibly, the pen was in his shirt pocket and clicked when he pressed Charlotte to his chest while strangling her. Hmm.

"Good morning, Phin," she greeted him and grabbed her own mail from her box, at the same time ending the recording of his clicking pen. Her greeting would serve as her label, she decided. She had no reason to suspect Phineas of Charlotte's murder, but he was the only faculty member she had actually seen in the building on the night of the murder. Also, he was up for tenure and from his conversation with Pamela that night, he appeared to be concerned about tenure. If he believed that Charlotte would not support his candidacy, maybe he killed her to further his career.

Peeking around the corner into Jane Marie's office, she saw that the secretary was busily typing away, but she stopped momentarily to wave a greeting to Pamela then returned to her super fast typing. Click-clack. Her fingers sped over the keys. Now there's a clicking noise, thought Pamela. Oh, what's the matter with me? She stopped abruptly. Oh, sure. Jane Marie strangled Charlotte to death and then blithely started typing away on the computer keyboard. Or if she pressed Charlotte forward as she was strangling her, Charlotte's body could have pushed on the computer keyboard and pressed several keys, causing the double-click noise. Surely, that was crazy. She was losing it.

Even so, just to be thorough, she made a brief recording of her secretary typing, along with a quick vocal label. She'd better get to her office and start on something constructive before she was declared a basket case. As far as she knew, Jane Marie had no motive to hurt Charlotte. She was terribly protective of Mitchell and might do something drastic to protect her boss—but murder?

Pamela started out of the office and decided to take the central staircase to the second floor--not her usual route. As she arrived at the first landing, she heard voices coming from the floor below. Bob Goodman and Arliss had just entered the stairwell from the animal wing and were intently involved in a discussion. They didn't notice her presence on the landing above--or anyone else's presence it appeared, if anyone had been there. Pamela couldn't make out exactly what they were saying; she assumed it was about the animals, but as Bob and Arliss moved into the small alcove under the staircase which afforded them some privacy, she noted that their voices diminished somewhat, and some other sounds--not of the talking variety-- took over.

The sound of keys on Bob's key chain--the ones to the animal cages, no doubt, caught her attention first. They made a sort of clicking noise. Quickly and quietly, she recorded the jangling keys. Bob was a genuine and sweet person. Pamela couldn't imagine him hurting anyone. However, he lived for that animal lab of his and it was drowning in financial woes—no thanks to Charlotte and her penchant for scattering her beneficence on all of her colleagues except Bob and the animal psychology program. Would he kill her for that? As Pamela listened to Bob's keys, other sounds caught her interest. This was flagrant eavesdropping, she realized, and she remained frozen in place. She felt terrible spying on Bob and Arliss like this, but couldn't help herself. Her temptation to peek over the railing was overwhelming and, as there appeared to be no one else around, she allowed herself a quick look.

There she saw her good friend Arliss and Dr. Bob Goodman standing very close together, leaning against the side of the staircase. Bob had one arm around Arliss' back and his face snuggled into her neck. Arliss did not look as if she minded this one bit.

"You looked so pretty yesterday at the chapel," cooed Bob.

"Oh, Bob," responded Arliss, in a sweet, soft voice that Pamela would never have imagined coming from Arliss's lips.

My God, thought Pamela. Arliss, you devil. And I thought I was the one with all the secrets. She quickly pulled back from her hidden position before the couple below noticed her on the staircase above. As soon as she'd tip-toed the rest of the way up the stairs to the second floor, she quickly added her vocal label for the sound of Bob's keys—leaving out any mention of the less metallic sounds of human smooching. Arliss had kept her little romance completely quiet all this time. If she was an accomplice to murder or even a murderer herself, would she be able to keep that quiet too? It was obvious that Arliss had no love for Charlotte and blamed her for the mess the animal lab was in. Pamela was still trying to digest her new discovery as she walked the slightly further distance to her office at the other end of the second floor hallway.

As she rounded the corner, she saw Joan in her office with a student. Pamela's tape recorder was still on record mode. Joan obviously had just arrived and was opening her briefcase while the student waited patiently. Pamela heard the briefcase click as it popped open. Now, she thought, there was a loud click. But was it the click on my murder tape? Oh, my, she thought. There's no way that Joan Bentley could have killed Charlotte. She may not have liked her any better than anyone else, but Joan was no killer, of that, Pamela was certain. Why would Joan kill Charlotte? Joan didn't seem to have a jealous bone in her body. Or did she? With Charlotte's death, Joan was now the Chair of the Tenure Committee, a very important position. Would she kill for that? Joan didn't even seem to be particularly annoyed by Charlotte, when everyone else was. Was her behavior all just an act? Of course not, Pamela was certain of that.

Just as she was certain that Arliss was not having an affair with Dr. Bob Goodman. Right. Where had she been all this time? Obviously, way too busy with her own concerns. She needed to stop all this paranoia about the killer and the disk and focus on what she was supposed to be doing. Her job. Her students. Her classes. However, turning towards her hidden mike, "Joan Bentley, briefcase," she said for the recorder.

She'd just entered her office when she heard another click-click sound. Something tapping the floor. This one she thought she remembered and, sure enough, Dr. Willard Swinton appeared momentarily in her door, leaning on his antique cane, its silver handle gleaming.

"I heard you coming, Willard," she teased, and unseen, clicked her recorder to stop, collecting both sound and label.

"No surprise visits for me, I guess," he responded jauntily. "I hope you had a relaxing weekend, Pamela. It was a lovely memorial service, wasn't it? Hopefully, we'll all be able to put the horrors of last week behind us and get back to business. I'd like to chat with you about your new study when you have time."

"Agreed," she nodded.

"Just call me, if you need anything," he confided, stepping into her office a bit.

"Thank you, Willard," she responded, putting her books and papers on her desk. He headed off down the hall towards his office, the metal tip of his cane, clicking and clacking on the floor. How could she even for a moment contemplate Willard as a murderer? He could barely get around, let alone strangle someone. But he was large, she noted. Maybe he was stronger than he looked. His only obvious difficulty was walking. As far as she knew, his arms worked just fine, maybe fine enough to strangle Charlotte.

She could hear Rex Tyson in the lecture hall next door, practicing. Leaving her office, she strolled into the large room. Rex was standing at the lectern in the front of the room. Inside the lectern, she knew, was a locked cabinet where the controls for the overhead projector were housed. She had watched Rex lecture several times; he always used pre-programmed computerized slides. He would walk around the classroom like a talk show host, changing the screen image as he went. She remembered now, seeing him change the slides with a remote control device.

"Dr. Barnes," he called out, as he noticed her watching him at the back of the room. "Here to watch me practice?"

"I don't know, Rex," she laughed, "Do you need to test some new jokes?"

"A few juicy ones, actually," he winked.

"Truth be told," she said, coming closer, "I was interested in that overhead projector. I might need it for my graduate seminar next week. Is it hard to use?"

"Nah," he responded, "Easy as pie. You just slip your slides in the tray under the lectern and you can run the whole thing with the remote from anywhere in the room."

"Really?"

"Yep," he said, drawing a small gray rectangular object from his shirt pocket. "Just one click for forward and two clicks for reverse." He demonstrated the device—and its sound--for her. Quietly, her finger pressed the correct button on the recorder in her pocket.

"That's great," she replied, "I'll see if I can gather enough slides to make it worth my while. Thanks, Rex." She clicked off her hidden recorder, turned, and started to leave.

"Any time, Pam," he sang out and went back to his practice session.

She went back to her office, closed her door, and dialed the main office extension on her the phone. Jane Marie answered at once.

"Psychology Department," she said sweetly.

"Jane Marie," said Pamela, "Who all in our department teaches in the large lecture class next to my office?"

"Let's see," said Jane Marie, thinking, "Dr. Tyson on Monday and, I don't think anyone else in our department on a regular basis. Sometimes faculty members take their classes there to use the projector from time to time—it's really great. I know Anthropology uses it too. Did you want to use that room, Dr. Barnes?"

"No," she responded quickly. "Jane Marie, who would have access to the projector remote control device for that room?"

"The remote is supposed to stay in the main office, Dr. Barnes. But, Dr. Tyson uses it the most often," she laughed, "so he usually carries it around with him—in his shirt pocket. If someone wanted to use it, they'd have to pluck it from his cold dead fingers. Oh, sorry, Dr. Barnes—bad joke."

"Don't be sorry," she chuckled, "I was just wondering. Bye." So, she thought, Rex could have strangled Charlotte, but why? Of the three candidates up for tenure, he seemed most likely to get it. Maybe he antagonized Charlotte with his pranks and grandstanding. She always liked to be the center of attention. It didn't seem likely, but at this point she was willing to entertain any idea.

Pamela scrounged in her side drawer until she found a connector cord so she could upload the data from the mini-recorder in her pocket, directly to her computer. She hooked the small device to her office mainframe. Bringing up both her acoustic program and the new data from her mini-recorder, she sat back in her desk chair and took a deep breath.

Soon, on the screen appeared her acoustic analysis program along with both the original data—that of Charlotte's murder—and now, this new data she had just made of the sounds she had surreptitiously recorded throughout the department. She marked the unique double-click sound from the murder recording clearly on the spectrograph with her cursor. Then, she played the new sounds she'd just recorded this morning in the second analysis line. As each clicking sound played, she froze its visual acoustic image on her screen for comparison with the double-click sound from the murder recording.

Thus, she listened to and visually compared the sounds. Some of the sounds were similar to, but none of them was a direct match—visually and auditorially—for the double-click sound on the murder recording she now knew so well. That is, not until she reached one particular sound.

That sound was—and it didn't even require her professional eye and ear to make this determination—a perfect match. The sounds were identical in audio features—pitch, intensity, and duration. The acoustic images were visually identical—two short, peaked waves. The enormity of her discovery overwhelmed her. Removing her hands from her keyboard, she leaned back in her desk chair, thinking. This was what she'd been looking for. The mysterious clicking noise on the murder disk. She now knew what caused it—and she knew who caused it. She knew who had killed Charlotte Clark. Now what? She sat there for several minutes frozen with uncertainty.

Then, with slow, but cold determination she lifted the receiver to her desk phone and dialed.

Chapter 23

The next afternoon, as Pamela was checking out for the day, she found herself standing in the main office by the mail boxes, where several faculty members were gathered chatting.

"Would you mind coming to my office for a minute?" she asked one of them. "I have a research problem I'd like to ask you about."

"Sure," was the response, "Just let me drop this stuff off at my office and I'll be right there."

"Great," she answered and quickly headed for her office up the central staircase.

Now, just minutes later, as she stood behind her desk waiting, her heart beating loudly, she thought over and over how frightened she was at this important moment--possibly, the most important moment in her life.

"Dr. Barnes?" Willard Swinton entered her office a few steps. "I thought you'd left for the day."

"Uh, Willard, yes. I...had to return...because I forgot something I needed at home."

"I hate it when that happens," he confided. "With my cane, it takes me forever to get from one location to the other. If I have to backtrack, it's really demoralizing."

"Yes, well, I've got what I needed," she said, standing motionless behind her desk.

"Good," he smiled. "Well, have a lovely evening, Pamela."

"You too." He turned and headed back to his office. Pamela stood at her desk, riveted. She looked down and took a deep breath. Too close. Simply too close.

Rex Tyson appeared at her door, leaning jauntily on the doorframe.

"So?" he spoke in a friendly manner, "What's up?"

She jerked her head up and gripped her desk tightly with both hands.

"About the overhead remote...."

"The remote again," he smiled. "That's your research problem?"

"Could I see how it works?" she asked sweetly. He pulled the device out of his shirt pocket and handed it to her. She examined the device and pressed it. Two clicks. Yes, the sound was identical.

"Actually," she said, "this is my research problem. Listen, will you?"

As she knew exactly where the cursor button was, she clicked it with her mouse without even looking down at her computer and the sound she now knew so well emerged at full volume from her speakers. Charlotte's choking voice unmistakable, her bumps, scrapes, scratches--and then, the double clicking noise that had revealed to her Rex's obvious involvement. Click-click. Pause. Then click-click again. She watched his reaction as she listened.

Rex's face turned white--as if the blood in his entire body had suddenly drained into a vessel beneath him—the instant he heard Charlotte's voice. It was obvious to Pamela that he'd heard this horrifying sound before—because, of course, he had. He said nothing, just stared at her, not moving even the slightest. When the recording stopped, Pamela spoke.

"I didn't know how to connect any of the sounds I was hearing to the killer. For all I knew, Charlotte made all those sounds herself in trying to get away. Then, I realized that the clicking noise was probably not a sound that came from Charlotte--in her effort to save herself from the killer. The clicking noise was probably made by the killer—probably inadvertently. So I started to look for that sound. I remembered seeing you use that remote for the projector and I thought it might be the noise on this tape. When Jane Marie informed me that you were the only faculty member who regularly uses the remote and that you carry it with you in your shirt pocket, I knew I'd found Charlotte's killer."

Rex continued to remain silent. She couldn't tell if he was going to speak or do anything. She waited.

"How?'" he finally muttered, trance-like.

"I don't really think how is the important question, Rex," she responded, "I think the more important question is why."

Rex slowly began to sense his surroundings. He glanced at Pamela, then at the door, and then around the room. Ever so slowly, he took a few steps towards her, raised his hand, reached behind him, and gently and quietly, closed her office door. Pamela was braced for this; she suspected he would not respond with remorse.

"Why?" he repeated her words in a husky whisper, as he moved carefully closer to her desk. "Why? I'll tell you, Miss Busybody. Because your buddy Charlotte Clark couldn't mind her own damn business, just like you. There was no reason for her to demand that we include our dissertations in our tenure portfolios. She just did that to ruin me. I knew it as soon as she made that requirement. It was evident that she wanted that Delmondo chick tenured over me--she's always been her pet. And when word got out that the Dean was only allowing two candidates to have tenure--I knew she was out to get me."

"But, Rex," said Pamela, her eyes never leaving his for a moment, "you were in an excellent position for tenure. Your publication record is stellar and actually far superior to Laura's."

He chuckled. "Well, not exactly. Let's just say that Phineas is a major part of my publication record," he noted mockingly.

"You mean you haven't contributed much to your articles with Phin?" she guessed.

"I am," he mused, continuing his slow progress forward, "shall we say--the front man. A position Phin used to appreciate, but hasn't seemed to value as much as he should--lately."

"The two of you must have been fighting because he doesn't feel it's fair for you to keep on being rewarded for his work. In other words, you shouldn't have ever gotten first author billing on any of your articles, right?"

"That little chump has the gall to think I should remove my name from consideration for tenure," he sneered.

So that was it, she thought, Phineas wasn't asking about the possibility of removing his name from consideration for tenure, he was asking about the possibility of removing Rex's name.

She said, "And I suppose Charlotte somehow figured out that the two of you were arguing about this, and she managed to put two and two together and determined that your credentials were—shall we say—less than sterling."

"Your precious Charlotte," he scowled, "just had to go and start digging around in places where she didn't belong, thanks to that damn subscription database."

"Just what did she discover?" asked Pamela, cautiously.

He shrugged, his eyes still in line with Pamela's. Suddenly, it all became clear—the Culver dissertation, the secret notebook.

"You--you plagiarized your dissertation, didn't you?" she exclaimed.

"Whatever," he scoffed, "It didn't matter. She would've made something up if she hadn't found what I'd pulled from Culver's dissertation. She wanted her precious Laura to get tenure. She always had to get her own way. When she came into my office Tuesday afternoon and told me exactly what she was going to do, what she suspected, and how she was going to track it down, jeez, it was like she was asking me to kill her." He spoke as if he believed Charlotte's murder was justified.

"And you were happy to oblige," responded Pamela.

"Of course," he smiled, getting closer to the desk and side-stepping his way around it towards Pamela, saying, "I'm always happy to oblige a lady." With that, he reached out towards her and grabbed her neck. Pamela pushed him back hard with both hands while at the same time screaming at the top of her lungs.

"You bitch!" he snarled, but he didn't let go. He struggled to gain a tighter hold as she pushed back hard and screamed again.

"Shut up!" he growled, shoving her backwards against her wall. Pamela frantically tried to extricate her neck from his grasp. Their struggle knocked over her desk chair. Pamela was becoming tired.

"Stop it!" he threatened. "I should've run you into a ditch Friday night and finished you off then!" He slammed her against the wall, pushing on her neck and upper body as hard as he could.

She was now unable to get her hands between his hands and her neck. Her cries were stopped by the pressure his large hands were placing on her throat.

When she believed she couldn't last one more second without air, she heard footsteps in the hallway, people calling her name, and the sound of her office door rattling.

Chapter 24

His hands pushed hard on her throat and his upper body pressed her into the wall. The back of her head was smashed up against a framed copy of her doctoral diploma. A lot of good this certificate did her now in fighting for her life, she thought.

Rex's cheek was a whisker away from hers as he growled into her ear, "You stupid bitch! Why couldn't you leave well enough alone?"

She was struggling for air and desperately trying to push him away. Sounds of people outside the door, yelling, and the door rattling wavered at the corner of her consciousness.

Rex seemed oblivious to the sounds in the hall. He was totally focused on squeezing the life out of her.

All of a sudden, the door exploded and slammed against the far wall—reverberating wildly. Shoop burst into the room, followed by several officers with guns drawn. Joan, Kent, and Willard were clumped in a group, peeking in from the hallway.

Rex grimaced as Shoop directed the officers to pull him away from Pamela, which they did, shoving him forcefully against the far wall. Joan ran into the room and put her arms around Pamela's shoulders and guided her to the sofa. Pamela was limp, shaking, her hands touching her throat, feeling for damage. Kent and Willard watched from the doorway.

"My God, Dr. Barnes! Are you all right?" called out Kent.

"Don't make her talk," said Joan, holding up a hand to Kent, "Her throat might be injured."

"Shall I call I doctor?" asked Kent.

"No," said Pamela, in a dry, choked voice, "I'm all right. Just scared."

"Cuff him," said Shoop to the officers, and the two men turned Rex around and pulled his arms behind him, quickly snapping handcuffs on his wrists.

"Kent," directed Joan, "why don't you go get Dr. Barnes a glass of water."

"A pitcher--in my refrigerator," Pamela spoke hoarsely, pointing her finger at her coffee cup on her desk. Kent grabbed the cup, went to the small icebox, and poured her a drink of water. She swallowed the liquid hungrily. It felt wonderful in her throat and cooling.

"Thank you," she said. "Thank you, all."

Detective Shoop spoke to her, looking somewhat sheepish.

"Dr. Barnes," he said, "Sorry it took us so long to get inside your office. We were all ready to go, hiding out in Dr. Bentley's office, but the bastard managed to lock your door. We should have planned better. That was too close."

"Detective Shoop," replied Pamela, now calmer and somewhat amused by the lanky man, "I'm just grateful you and your men were here as my---my back-up, as you say. Anyway, we at least have proof that Dr. Tyson murdered Dr. Clark now."

"You have nothing!" cried Rex.

"Actually, Rex," she said, turning to where he stood handcuffed, "I do," and she drew the tiny hand-held tape-recorder from her pocket. "I have your entire confession right here."

"Dr. Barnes, I guess we're going to have to put you on the payroll," noted Shoop. All right, everyone, let's all get out of here and give Dr. Barnes a chance to catch her breath. The officers will take care of---the suspect. I had my doubts about you, Tyson right from the git go. Anyway, men, get him out of here."

The police officers quickly dragged Rex out of Pamela's office.

"My dear," whispered Joan to Pamela, "This has been a day to remember. You catch the killer and I get locked in my office with three hunky police men." She gave her a quick hug and then led Willard and Kent out of the office and down the hallway.

Pamela found herself alone with Shoop. She was seated on the sofa, wondering if the man would manage to extricate her from her comfortable position, so he could lounge on her couch again. However, Shoop remained standing.

"So, Dr. Barnes," he said, peering down at her, "You solved the murder, it appears." He stared at her intently.

She heard small footsteps running down the hall. Angela appeared in the doorway breathless.

"Mom!" she cried, running to her mother on the couch and hugging her tightly, "Are you okay? Kent said someone tried to kill you."

"I'm fine, sweetheart," she replied, enjoying every second of a very infrequent hug from her daughter. "This is Detective Shoop, who's investigating the case. Detective, my daughter Angela."

The big detective bowed courteously to the young woman. Angela, oblivious, turned to her mother.

"Mom," she begged, "This is terrible. You should go home."

"I'm afraid, dear," shrugged Pamela, "that the detective needs to question me about what happened."

"Can't you wait until tomorrow?" Angela demanded of the detective. Pamela was delighted to see her daughter defend her so strongly. This was the most affection she had shown her in ages and Pamela was enjoying every moment of it.

"Hmmm," he sighed, realizing that it was probably hopeless to accomplish much at the moment. "Dr. Barnes, if you'd be so kind as to come down to headquarters tomorrow and give us your statement, I guess we can let you go home. You've been through quite a bit today, and it does appear that you're no longer in any immediate danger."

"That would be wonderful," she smiled sweetly at him. He tucked his notebook back in his pocket and shook hands with both women and then departed quickly.

"Mom," repeated Angela, giving her mother a quick hug, "I can't believe all this. You're like a hero--or something." A hug too! Will wonders never cease?

"Actually," noted Pamela, "Jane Marie, Joan, Willard, and Kent were here too. They followed the police in when Rex was trying to kill me."

"You mean Kent saved your life?"

"Sort of. He certainly did help." She noted how impressed her daughter was with this new accolade draped over the shoulders of the obviously remarkable Kent.

"Wow!"

"Tell you what," she hugged her daughter warmly, "Let's get out of here."

The two—mother and daughter--headed out. Pamela stopped briefly in the main office to grab her mail and to let Jane Marie know she was leaving.

As she entered Jane Marie's small alcove, she discovered a mob of people gathered--Kent, Willard, Phineas, Joan, Laura, Bob, Arliss, and several other graduate students—almost the entire department. Actually, they were all standing around Jane Marie's desk, as Jane Marie described what had happened between Rex and Pamela. When Pamela entered, they all parted way for her, all expressing concern. Obviously, Jane Marie was the source to go to for the latest scoop on this departmental excitement. Angela stood back from the group of faculty and watched while her mother became the center of attention.

Joan gave Pamela an especially long squeeze. Arliss hugged her too.

"'Same 'ol, same 'ol,' my foot," Pamela whispered to Arliss, returning the hug. Arliss gave her a look of confusion, and Pamela nodded slyly in the direction of Bob Goodman, at which Arliss blushed deeply, "You can certainly keep a secret."

The others shook her hand, patted her on the back or hugged her. She felt a tremendous amount of love from her colleagues.

At that moment, Mitchell's door opened and the department head called to her.

"Dr. Barnes," he cried, "Thank God, you're all right! If you don't mind, I'd really like to speak with you about all of this--just for a moment." He awaited her response, which he assumed would be for her to enter his office.

"Um, Mitchell," she hesitated, "my daughter Angela is with me. I promised her I'd take her home.... "

"I'll be glad to take Angie home, Dr. Barnes," spoke up Kent, who was chatting quietly with Angela towards the back of the well-wishers.

"Wonderful!" announced Mitchell, and grabbed Pamela's elbow and escorted her into his office. Pamela looked back at her daughter, who waved a friendly good-bye as she headed out with Kent at her side.

"Jane Marie," begged Pamela, "would you please call my husband and tell him I'll be a bit late and why?"

"Sure, Dr. Barnes." She gave Pamela a heartfelt look of sympathy.

The pack of faculty members dissipated with Pamela's disappearance into Mitchell's inner sanctum.

Mitchell gestured for Pamela to sit and took his royal place at his large desk.

"My God!" he said, shaking his head, "I can't believe all of this has happened. Your life was threatened. And Rex. He's such a cheerful, good-natured guy. Lord, he has a wife and two small children. It never crossed my mind that he was capable of such a thing."

"Me neither," she answered, "But it's over now. It's really over, Mitchell. The killer's been caught and we don't have to be frightened anymore."

"Yes," he said, sighing. "What a devastating thing for you-- for us—for the department."

"I know," she replied, "To lose two faculty members in such a terrible way."

They were both silent for a moment.

"Pamela," he then said, carefully, "Jane Marie told me how worried you and she have been about certain things that have happened recently—in addition, of course, to Charlotte's murder. Given what you've just gone through, I think you have a right to know something. It's something I've already told Jane Marie. But, I'd just ask that you keep what I'm going to tell you private."

"Of course," she replied, suddenly intrigued.

"First, let me say, I had no love for Charlotte. She aggravated me as I know she did many faculty here. But, Lord, I'd never contemplate hurting her or anything like that. Even so, Jane Marie apparently was worried about me and Charlotte--or my relationship with Charlotte. Evidently, she was concerned about an argument we'd had the day before the murder. I told her, and I'll tell you, the subject of that argument was the Tenure Committee. It's not really a secret. The Dean's demanding that we restrict tenure to two candidates rather than three."

Mitchell pulled his chair closer to his desk and bent in towards Pamela. "Look, I don't like this any better than anyone else, but there's not much I can do about it, and I told Charlotte that. She was furious with me--and the Dean--and just about everyone. She is—was--determined to have her own way and get Laura tenured. I told her Laura might be better off postponing applying for tenure until next year, and that Rex and Phin were, in my opinion, the two obvious candidates--although I don't vote on the committee. This made her even madder. We just both lost it. I'm so sorry now in retrospect. Anyway, I had no idea how far she'd go to seek vengeance, but evidently, she not only attempted to ruin Rex to prevent him from getting tenure--and he, as we know, took direct steps to do something about it, but--she also attempted to blackmail me."

"Blackmail?"

"Yes, Jane Marie told me that she--and you--know about the photograph of the woman Charlotte left in my mailbox. This is the private part. Oh, God, I'm so sorry. That photo is of a lovely young woman--Evelyn Carrier--a former student. I ran into her a few years ago at a convention and we got to talking-- and, this is embarrassing, Pamela--things were not going well between Velma and me at the time--and Evelyn and I became involved." Mitchell bent his head and ran his fingers through his blonde hair.

"Worse yet, it continued," he said. "Charlotte found out about it--I don't know how, but obviously she must have assumed that by showing me Evelyn's photo that I'd be frightened of exposure and side with her in support of Laura over Rex. She was wrong. All her actions did were to make me realize how dastardly my behavior had been. I confessed to Velma. Thank the Lord, she believed me when I said I was sorry, and that I wanted to work things out with her." He bit his lower lip and took a deep breath.

"I called Evelyn into my office and told her what had happened. I told her we'd no longer be able to see each other. She was sad, as Jane Marie saw when she witnessed Evelyn leaving my office, but it had to be done. Never once, did it occur to me to do anything to Charlotte. That's the whole story, Pamela. I hope hearing this doesn't forever demean me in your eyes."

"Actually, Mitchell," Pamela smiled warmly, "It just makes you seem human." He smiled back at her, his shoulders dropping noticeably.

"After this all calms down and things get back to normal," he mused, "I'll have to make adjustments to compensate for the loss of Charlotte and Rex in the department. Obviously, we'll have to hire replacements, but right now, I'll need to find a way to restructure our schedule to cover their classes in the mean time."

"If I may make a suggestion," she said.

"Pamela, given your involvement in all of this—and a positive one, if I may say so, I would truly value your input on how best to handle the void caused by Charlotte's and Rex's—um--absence."

"Mitchell," she began, "I know your first instinct is to replace Charlotte, but, really, when you think about it, you can't replace her. Students took her courses because she was who she was. Her subject area is so narrow, that to find someone of her caliber in the same field would be cost prohibitive. In Rex's case--well, Phin is a Rex clone. Not as good a teacher, but I think he's getting better. I would, for the rest of the semester anyway, to test the waters, have Phin take over Rex's upper division courses."

"And his two mass lecture classes?" he asked.

"Hmm," she smiled, "Seems to me we have an ideal person in our department, someone noted for their ability to handle general introductory courses--especially for undergrads--someone who even has published extensively. Now, it might be difficult to entice this person to pull himself away from administrative duties for the two hours on Mondays that he'd have to...."

"You are devious," mused Mitchell, "I do miss teaching. It's even possible that such an arrangement could be permanent. However, if we don't replace Rex or Charlotte, we'll have funding for two additional faculty lines. What would we do with that?"

"Mitchell," she teased, "You've been promising Bob Goodman increased funding for animal psychology for years and so has the Dean. You know that the animal lab is disintegrating and if it doesn't get a fresh influx of funds soon, you might just as well cancel animal psychology classes together. It seems to me that this is a golden opportunity to salvage our animal psych program--sort of an endowment from Charlotte--and Rex, if you will."

"Funny," he laughed, "Charlotte hated animal psych."

"Well," said Pamela, "She doesn't need to know."

"Are you sure you wouldn't like my job?" he asked.

"Never in a million years," she responded. They both laughed and she felt a new understanding of her typically inscrutable boss. He would never be her friend, but she could communicate with him, she realized. She bid him farewell and headed home.

Chapter 25

Rocky was, as usual, waiting for her at the kitchen door, a look of annoyance on his face. Jane Marie had phoned and informed him of the occurrences that took place in Pamela's office this afternoon. It would not be pretty, she knew. She had done everything he warned her not too. She was not an obedient spouse. She'd probably get latrine duty.

"Babe," he cried, embracing her tightly. She remained in his arms as long as she could. She knew there would be a scolding.

When she finally pulled away, she asked, "Well, aren't you going to make me do forty push-ups?"

"No," he said, softly, "It's a waste of time. I've resigned myself to the fact that I have a daredevil for a wife. Tracking down and confronting cold-blooded killers unarmed. No, not going to even mention the foolishness of such actions, because it's obvious that my wife pays absolutely no attention to any of my warnings."

"The police were there all the time," she gulped bravely. "It was a set-up."

"And you were the bait."

A soft-spoken Rocky was scarier than a furious Rocky. At least, she was used to his being macho and wanting to protect her. Maybe they truly were in a new era where men and women, husbands and wives, were each responsible for themselves--and each other.

"It's just that I--I--had evidence of the crime and I knew how to make use of it to find who killed Charlotte. I just couldn't ignore it."

"I know."

Candide appeared from around the corner. He had heard his mistress's voice and came prancing in, wanting a scratch. Pamela obliged.

"Did Angie get home yet?" she asked her husband.

"Yup," he responded, "She dropped off her books, introduced me to that macabre Kent fellow who looks like something out of a horror movie, told me her mother had almost been killed by a maniac, then they took off in his car."

"Rocky," she smiled, "I told you Kent is perfectly harmless."

"Isn't that what you used to think about that Rex fellow who attacked you this afternoon in your office?" he responded, teeth clenched.

"Please, honey," she pleaded, "I'll explain everything." She pulled on his arm. "Maybe, you could give me another one of your relaxing foot massages," she hinted.

"Don't you want dinner?" he asked.

"Yes," she responded, hopefully.

"I didn't make anything," he announced, looking glum.

"What? You didn't cook anything?" Had Hell frozen over?

"When your secretary called about you, I couldn't even think straight. Cooking was the last thing on my mind. I don't believe I'll be able to think about cooking ever again unless you promise me you'll give up sleuthing" he said, peering deep into her eyes.

"Sleuthing?" she questioned, stunned. "Well, of course, I can promise that. My sleuthing days are over."

"Wonderful," he replied, "Then, you've got your cook back."

She hugged him. She meant every word of her promise. She did. What was the likelihood that someone else would be murdered in their little town? What was the likelihood that even if that happened she would be the only one with the expertise to solve it? Virtually nil. Yes, it was an easy promise to make.

"Let's eat," said Rocky. As he led her into the dining room, she realized his threat had been a ruse. He'd prepared all her favorite dishes and the dining room table was gleaming with candles.

"You devil," she pouted, "You tricked me."

"How does it feel?" he said, smiling

She breathed in the heavenly aroma and proceeded to nibble on his ear. "It feels wonderful," she whispered.

"Maybe an appetizer in the bedroom?"

"Sounds good."

"No," he said, putting his finger over her lips, "Absolutely no talk about sound tonight. And no talk about murder." With that, he scooped her up in his arms and they disappeared into the bedroom.

Rocky's Recipes

Comfort Cocoa

2 TB. Sugar
4 tsp. unsweetened cocoa powder
1 C. milk
¼ tsp. vanilla
½ C. skim milk (for topping)

Rocky mixes the sugar and cocoa powder with a bit of the milk and the vanilla, forming a paste in a saucepan. Then he slowly adds the rest of the milk and heats it on the stove until almost (but not quite) boiling. After putting the finished cocoa in the serving cup, he prepares a foam topping of ½ cup skim milk (which works best for foam) in a small saucepan. He heats the milk while foaming it with a handheld latte foamer until the milk is light and frothy. He tops the finished cup of cocoa with the foam and a sprinkling of shaved chocolate or cinnamon.

Sergeant's Stew

1 lb. beef stew meat
1 onion
1 clove garlic
1 potato
1 carrot
1 celery stalk
1 small can of peas
1 medium can of diced tomatoes
1 cup of red wine
1 16-oz container of chicken stock
1 tsp. Italian seasoning
2 TB.steak sauce
2 TB olive oil

Rocky sautés the stew meat in a TB of olive oil in a large frying pan until browned on all sides. Then he adds the red wine and simmers for 20 minutes. While waiting, Rocky next chops the onion and garlic clove and sautés them together in a TB of olive oil in a separate pan over medium heat until soft and brown. Then, he peels the potato and carrot. He chops the potato, carrot, and celery stalk into small chunks. Finally, he places all remaining ingredients in a large stew pot, and adds water if necessary to cover the raw vegetables. He lets the stew simmer on the stove for three or four hours, stirring occasionally.

Italian Sausage Soup

1 lb. Italian sausage
1 onion
1 clove garlic
1 tsp. Italian seasoning
1 cup white wine
1 16-oz. container chicken stock
1 large potato
1 cup fresh spinach
fresh grated parmesan cheese

Rocky first removes the sausage from the casings and sautés it in a frying pan. He chops the onion and garlic finely and sautés them in a separate pan until golden brown. He peels and chops the potato into small chunks. Eventually, he puts all ingredients except the cheese into a large pot and lets them simmer on the stovetop for several hours. He sprinkles the cheese over each bowl just before serving.

Patricia Rockwell has spent most of her life teaching. From small liberal arts colleges to large regional research universities—and even a brief stint in a high school, her background in education is extensive. She has taught virtually everything related to Communication—from a fine arts speech-theatre orientation to more recently a social science research approach. Her Bachelors' and Masters' degrees are from the University of Nebraska in Speech, and her Ph.D. is from the University of Arizona in Communication. She was on the faculty at the University of Louisiana at Lafayette for thirteen years, retiring in 2007.

Her publications are extensive, with over 20 peer-reviewed articles in scholarly journals, several textbooks, and a research book on her major interest area of sarcasm, published by Edwin Mellen Press. In addition to publications, she has presented numerous papers at academic conferences and served for eight years as Editor of the *Louisiana Communication Journal*. Her research focuses primarily on several areas of communication: deception, sarcasm, and vocal cues.

Dr. Rockwell is presently living in Aurora, Illinois, with her husband Milt, also a retired educator. The couple has two adult children, Alex and Cecilia.

9501334R0